A Dissertation Upon Second Fiddles

Vincent O'Sullivan

Solis Press

Originally published in 1902 by Grant Richards, London. This edition completely reset with minor spelling changes and published in 2020 by Solis Press

ISBN: 978-1-910146-45-3

Published by Solis Press, PO Box 482,
Tunbridge Wells TN2 9QT, Kent, England

Web: www.solispress.com | *Twitter*: @SolisPress

Contents

℮

Section I

OF KINDRED

Chapter I

THE LIVES OF THOSE who have benefited mankind are often read with interest, even by men who have no touch of the liberal virtues; for men like to watch the rise of actions which they themselves would by no means perform. And so I count to give you pleasure while now I relate the history of the philanthropist, Sir Hugh Anger, whose case was indeed an example of great variety of fortune; for through a part of his life he was happy, inasmuch as he did what he liked, but at the end he was matter for tragedy.

You must know that this Sir Hugh Anger was of a large and corpulent presence, and he loved a good wine and good meat as well as any man in the kingdom, or out of it. In deed, his devotion to these dainties, and to creamy dainties in silk, had cast him into the hands of doctors who, after a while, became the only people that occupied his thoughts. He had fallen in some years from the lusty health of a sea-man to a pitiable examination of each twitch of his muscles; his chief apprehension was death; and the least sting of an indigestion would send him on a hop to a doctor. He had one doctor for his head, another for his heart, and a third for his middle parts; and you might see his brougham almost any day of the week in front of a house in Harley Street or Cavendish Square. The large expense of money which this put him to, he did not complain of, although he liked not giving; for he was that subtle kind of miser who is his own darling prodigal; and he would squander on himself, while he would haggle over a groat whereof the spending could buy him no pleasure. And if he was ever betrayed by weakness into an action so much against his stomach as to give money which brought him no advantage, he yet had the advantage which lies in the pleasure of parading your charity on your arm out of doors; and he would boast of his munificence in his clubs enough to glut his hearers. This propensity of his became so well marked that he was driven to his shifts, after a while, to get an ear; and as he liked to declare in a genial company that he had small belief in friends—who can be surprised that his acquaintance dropped off one by one. But this last troubled him little; for he was, in sooth, of so wily and suspicious a temper that he could not distinguish a friend from a suitor. He agreed with King Harry the VIIIth that if he thought his cap knew his counsel he would cast it into the fire and burn it; and he had often in his mouth the king's shrewd saying: "Three may keep counsel, if two be away." His best friend, he was wont to say when he was merry, died young. Even in his amours, the particular mignonnes of his fancy soon found that they had much more need of him than he ever had of them; and his yaws between lechery and avarice were hard to support with a dimpled face. For when he had for the nonce exhausted the satisfactions of the town, and the thought of his health, never very remote, again got the upper hand, he retired into the country, and there, surrounded by a great retinue of servants, he lived solitary, a reversed Carthusian, wrapped in a gross, material, and degraded meditation on death. Holding his pulse, scanning his tongue, noting the coloration of his skin, so he passed vacantly the hours. And not seldom after he had dined heartily, he would wake up in the middle of the night with his heart flying, his cheeks on fire, and the terror of a lonely death in his soul, and thereupon the household would be dragged from their beds, and a groom sent clattering off to the village for the doctor.

Chapter II

He was in his most melancholy and vapourish mood the night the German came. It was a night of clamorous wind and rain; and Sir Hugh had taken a good whack at the wine after dinner to keep himself in spirits, and then had moved to the library, and in a large chair set before the fire, had dropped into a thick sleep. From this he had been awake about half-an-hour, and all his late exhilaration gone, was sitting with a flushed countenance and dull eyes staring dejectedly at an unopened copy of *The Times* on his knee, when a slight pale gentleman in spectacles, who had the grave airs of a professor, followed the servant on the scene.

Sir Hugh rose with a mien of surprise at so late a visit from a stranger; but he would have welcomed an interruption of the Devil himself as a relief from the heaviness which lay upon him. The German met his eye without a trace of uneasiness, and remarked the inclement weather.

"It spoils a man's clothes," he said.

"Yes, yes," replied Sir Hugh. "In this part of the country—and that—we have rain, you know—in and all that—well, a good three-parts of the year."

"I see that you cannot be insolent," quoth the gentleman. "You doubtless remarked the cut of Munich in my clothes, and another might have let fly a back-handed gibe at my thinking about such clothes at all. But you, sir, I am assured, come from a stock of quiet ladies and honest, clean-spoken men: you have an inheritance of courtesy, and it is not in your power to be insolent. Believe me, sir, that where you find insolence, I don't care how high the family may be placed, the kitchen is not for nothing in the breeding."

"This fellow talks like a book," thought Sir Hugh. "What a lot of rubbish about nothing! I never looked at his clothes. I've something else to think about," and he felt his stomach.

"You find this climate agrees with you?" asked the stranger.

"Oh yes, yes, perfectly," said Sir Hugh. "I know people say about damp—and that—you know everybody doesn't—just alike in these matters—and so—it may be, perhaps—but I'm bound to say it suits me."

The German had placed himself in an arm-chair, and bringing the tips of his fingers together, he regarded Sir Hugh with disapproval. "And yet," he observed in a cold tone, "it seems to me that you are not well."

"God bless my soul!" cried Sir Hugh with a jump. "Not well? I'm as well as ever I was in my life. Do I look ill?" he cried, with his hand on the bell. "I'll tell you what it is," says Sir Hugh, very warm, "I don't take it kind of you—not kind at all—to come to my house—yes, my house and all that—and—and so—in short, to frighten the wits out of me."

"I don't say that I find you ill," replied the other very soberly, "but I detect that your mind is not at ease. Your chief thought—your only thought really—is how to save your life, and you know you cannot save it from death. This thought appals you and keeps you sweating. Is it not true?"

"True!" exclaimed Sir Hugh. "True! I should think it was. You'll find people going about and whining" (here he put on a mincing mawkish air) "of the joy to be dissolved and to be with Christ, but I can assure you I'm not one of 'em. It's wonderful, when I come to think of it, how little desire I have to go to Heaven. Why there now—there's my neighbour Thorganby whom I knew as great a wencher—but it's no use to go into that. All I know is that I'm getting on—wear very well of course—strong and hearty, thank Heaven—could jump over the moon, and all that;—but still the years—*eheu fugaces,* as what's-his-name says in the book—very neat too—quite brilliant in fact—and so—and so—eh, what, what?—well, I find the years keep piling up on the wrong side, and I'd do anything to stop 'em—anything. I once read, I don't know where, of a man who was being cut—most horrible!" cried Sir Hugh in a flash of nervousness, "wish I hadn't thought of it at this time of night—but cut and all that—yes, cut for the dropsy,—yelling to the surgeon to cut deeper; and I'm sure I can understand it—or something like it at any rate. Not very religious perhaps, not what you call—"

"Your man was Samuel Johnson," put in the German. "But he—"

"I don't know who it was," quoth Sir Hugh. "But he had the right sow by the ear, as the king said—and no doubt you were going to say."

"I was going to say," resumed the stranger, "that he had not the means to prolong life which you have. He indeed loved his life and abhorred death, but he was a poor man. Now, you are a rich man."

"I rich!" cried Sir Hugh uneasily, who now began to smell a suitor. "Rich? Not at all, not at all. I am, in fact, as the world goes, very poor—and that—not at all well off. Why, the other day I was talking to—but we'll say nothing about that—but—and so—in short, I had to let the Moor Farm go for a trifle—an old sing-song."

"I don't want any of your money," replied the other coldly; "the sooner you get that into your head the better. But you are truly a rich man: it is necessary for my argument to allow that, so if you please we will take it for granted. Now, have you ever considered the effect of other people's wishes on your own life?"

"No," answered Sir Hugh with a chuckle, for he was grown mighty easy now that he saw he had not affair with a beggar. "No, I can't say I have. Never in all my days. No, sir."

Chapter III

"It has been observed in divers ages," began the German, "that statesmen in popular states, and others who work in the public eye, have been most happy and fortunate in their dealings when they have a great force of good-will from a multitude of people; but on the other side, when they excite the envy and ill-wishes of a good number, they fall irresolute and unlucky, not only in affairs of state, where popular feeling has influence, but in particular matters with which the populace has nothing to do. So the politic man notes it with joy, if the popular wind blows in his favour, even when he enterprises things private. Commanders, too, do well to extinguish envy by attributing their success to Providence or Fortune, rather than their own wits; for though the commander have the good-will of his army when he fights and wins his battles, yet he must gain the hearts of that greater army, the people, lest the favour of the first be outweighed by the malevolence of the last. Indeed, it has been well noted that after great triumphs men have been ill-disposed for some days following; and this because of the *oculus malus*, or wicked envious spyings which have been cast upon them out of the crowd. And to go some steps down, certain it is that a youth at school who has wrenched a coveted prize from his mates, is often overcome by a strange languor, which he takes from the malign, poisonous, and oblique eyes of those he has dejected. And as for princes, their inner spirits are more contented, and they sit easier on their thrones, their lives, too, in general are longer, when the greatest part of their subjects are not indifferent (I do not say hostile, which would be another matter, and not so good for my argument)—I say, rather, when the mass of subjects are not indifferent, but wish their prince heartily well: and this is true even in cases where the throne is stayed and buttressed by a great army, and there is no question of rebellion. Napoleon lost the good-will of the majority after the Russian disaster; until that time his ill-wishers were the minority, and from that time he began to go down; and his fall would have been swifter if the strong good-will of the soldiers had not for a while resisted the concentrated ill-will of the people. But at the end the side whereon the greatest number of wills were massed, conquered. And Napoleon, you will note, had the will of the people with him from the beginning; for when he came in the people were framed by the Revolution, and as he was a part and product of the Revolution, he mingled well with the country, which after was content to be led whither he would go. But for a legitimate prince, till he has reigned a number of years, it must depend on his predecessor whether his subjects are favourable, or hostile, or indifferent; since it is a truth much neglected, that princes inherit a kingdom the temper of which has been created by the preceding monarch. So it will be found most difficult to unthrone a bad prince who has followed a good and strong one; while a humane prince coming after a tyrant or a fool can easily be brought to the dust. The Revolution in France was made by the people of Louis XV., not by the people of Louis XVI.; and if Louis XVI. had come before Louis XV. perhaps the storm would not have arisen, at least in his successor's reign. In Queen Victoria's time there was an example of two peoples: for, when that Queen came first to the Crown she had subjects indifferent and murmuring whom she had inherited from the Georges and King William; but as she continued to live, she formed her own subjects and gained their good-will to such a point, that throughout her reign there was never the least attempt made on the throne,—no, nor any considerable whisper of faction. And I would hazard" (says the stranger, eyeing Sir Hugh) "that the accumulated force of will her subjects put forth that she should live, brought her to the great age at which she died.

"Here I touch the point I have been striving for, which is the effect of the will of a number of people to prolong or abbreviate life. For if a sovereign, or statesman, who is favoured lasts longer, as a rule, and in his private ways is happier, than one who is abhorred; cannot the same be said of particular retired men? But it falls to be noted that such keen hatred, or enough to do much harm, is never vented on the private man, as upon him who is mingled in high public affairs, unless there be found a good sum of people, relations or other, who with concentrated and undistracted wills desire the termination of his life, because they look to profit by his death. These hawks, you will find, do often attend men rich and of great estate; though it cannot be questioned that men—ay, and women too, who are tyrannical and oppressive in their families, are often brought down to the grave by the wishes of their company, who look for no reward other than a relief from the tyrant's clamours;—but the hawks who smell gold are strongest, unrelenting and most ruthless, and they surround the heads of the rich. What then can equal the folly of the rich man who announces to the world that he has bestowed large sums upon this one and that in his will; since poor fool! instead of receiving blessings for his act, as he fondly supposes, he begets in each one who is to benefit, a wish more or less strong for his dissolution. A first principle of long lasting for a rich man is to go about proclaiming that he has not left a groat or a stiver to anybody. A second principle (and here I beseech your attention) is to arrange that a certain number of people shall suffer grievously and cruelly at his death; who, therefore, from a consideration of their own interest, which is the only secure handle wherewith you can swing mankind, will heartily wish he may remain alive. Your rich man, in effect, instead of giving annuities that begin with his death, should give annuities that cease with his life. Seek out then, sir, I implore you, your indigent relatives, and some others poverty-stricken, who are also obstinate and tenacious in their thoughts; raise them to comfort, even to opulence, and let them understand that at the moment of your death they sink back into their original misery. You will thus form, to keep you alive, a mass of will-power, proceeding from obstinate, self-absorbed, strong-minded men and women, whose constant wish will be for you to remain on earth, and whose greatest dread and misfortune will be to hear of your death. And as I conclude, I would add a word of caution. In choosing those who are to enjoy your bounty, choose not those lost in the depths of poverty, the patent mendicants; but choose rather those men, and above all, those women, who live in a way and with a circumstance they have not the money to support; who ache to emulate some neighbour, but have not the wings to carry them: for it is people such as they who accept money with the lustiest greed, and who fall the sorest if it be withdrawn. As they have a greater knowledge and means of gratification, so have they a greater hunger, than the wretch who dreams perilous dreams in the parks, or ponders sad litanies in workhouses."

Upon that word, the German rose out of his chair, and going over to a table whereon were set some bottles and glasses, he filled a tumbler with soda-water and took it down at a gulp. Sir Hugh, meanwhile, sat watching him, twiddling his thumbs, and revolving as much as he could remember of what he had heard. He was, in truth, greatly engaged with this new Elixir of Life, and determined to put it on trial at once. But as his manner was, he beat about the bush.

"There's a good deal in what you say," he observed, "a good deal of sense—and that—and (by your leave) a good deal of moonshine too. You ask me to spend a heap of money on a lot of people I should be glad to see hanged—a power of money, mark ye,—and when I have dug a good hole in my pocket—and all that—squandered, so to speak—by the Lord! I may find myself no better than I was before. And so, as the fellow says,—I used to construe it out of the book when I was at school—shows how good my memory is, thank God!—no flaw there, what, what?—fine and strong, eh?—but, says he, a low, stupid man is the worst kind of madman."

The stranger gentleman appeared to take it ill that his proposals were received with so little enthusiasm. He looked at Sir Hugh in a way that made him quake. "It is of no interest to me whatever," he said in the tone of one who has endured an affront, "whether you follow my advice or not. If you do follow it, let me tell you it will be the best day's work you ever did in your life. I suppose you have made a will?" he asked menacingly.

"I have, yes indeed I have," answered Sir Hugh, uneasily shifting about. "Why, bless my life! I've made six in one way or other, if it comes to that," said he.

"And you have doubtless told people that they might look to benefit by your will?"

"Yes, I've let them know; and I've let 'em know when I've cut 'em out too—at times, sir, at times."

"Then consider," says the other solemnly, holding out his hand, "how many people there are, strong-willed, obstinate as bull-dogs, with the quenchless passion of greed on fire in their hearts, who are occupied at this very moment in wishing with all their force that you were in your coffin to-night."

"I do consider it, I do!" cried Sir Hugh, shaking like a flag. Chiefly there rose up in his mind a vision of a certain lady, a cousin of his, which he was unable to regard without terror. He resolved, therefore, to parry no longer, and acquainted the German that he was ready to follow his counsel.

"But perhaps you will allow me to inquire," he continued—"you know, without fashions and all that—why you bestow the advantage of your advice—of course it's very good of you, and that—but why you come to me, of all persons, at this hour of the evening to give me your assistance, since—well, in short, since I've never seen or heard of you before in my life."

The German smiled without mirth. "That is a matter which can only concern myself," he said. "Perhaps I acted on the principle of charity; perhaps I wanted to try an experiment. It were useless to speculate; for as to the designs of men, and the true reasons of their acting, we are in the world like gamesters seated round a table, who have indeed the whole pack distributed amongst them, yet not one can tell with any certainty more than his own hand.—And now," be added, "I will wish you a good night, good health, good cheer, and a good life, all of which you can derive from my precepts, except the first. Here upon this card I have written an address where you can come if you ever feel the need to consult me. And at the risk," said the German, "of appearing to impart useful information, and of a descent to the indoctrinating manners of the pedagogue" (a descent which, to do him bare justice, he seemed unconscious he had made more than once in the last hour), "I would ask you to remember, it was a very wise man who declared, that mankind places before all arts, and skill, or any distraction in the world, the hope of gain." And upon that he prepared to depart.

Sir Hugh urged him not to go further, and would have him lie at his house for the night; but the gentleman protested that he was engaged for the Continent in the morning, and with a deep bow he took his leave.

Chapter IV

The lady, Sir Hugh Anger's cousin, whom I just touched upon above, was no one else than Mrs Camilla Normansel; of whom it may well be said, that her calamities she owed to the foolishness of others, but for the fortitude with which she supported them she had to thank only God and herself: and it was a mark of her character that at the rare times when she found herself in a thankful mood, she was disposed to confine her thanksgiving to the earth. She had been married with a pretty good fortune to an officer of the army; and him she had followed to Ireland, to Gibraltar, to Malta, and other posts and places which those familiar with the movements of the British army will easily recall; till at last her husband, who for so young a man had shown a prodigious knowledge of strange ways to get rid of money, and had in a singularly brief time gone pretty well through her fortune, and his own to boot;—but at last, I say, he died one summer's morning of a dysentery, and she was left to find her way back to England with three children at her skirts. She had, thereupon, written to her kinsman, Sir Hugh, and had received from him a reply which made her face bright with rage. She folded the letter, and put it carefully away; and whenever she wanted to rouse in herself a storm of hate, it was her use to take it out and read it aloud. Sir Hugh had, in fact, told her with great suavity that he had found for her a corner in his will, and that by consequence he expected to be spared her importunities, and those of the rest of his relations, for as long as he remained in the world; which he confidently trusted would be for a good spell of years. The poor Mrs Normansel, then, had nothing left but to retire to a disgusting country town called Bridgwater, in the county of Somerset, and there she has been living, as good as bad, for four or five years, in that most depressing of all known states of life which people call genteel poverty, when Sir Hugh took a journey from town to apprize her of his new resolution for her convenience.

Before this, he had made his dispositions for the comfort of some other relatives and pensioners; but as he had a great fear of Camilla, and from that reason was decided to do more for her than for the rest, he had left her to the last: and now as he stood in the little parlour of a horrible little red-brick house in a row, before an empty grate, a vivid remembrance of this cousin of his, whom he had known from her birth and steered clear of whenever he could, rose in his mind, and he felt glad, for his own sake, that he had apportioned her the largest share of his bounty.

As he was thus reflecting, Mrs Normansel, dressed with great propriety, came into the room; and Sir Hugh ran her over with the cultured eye of an epicure. "What a figure she has!" he thought to himself. "She would be really a monstrous fine woman if it wasn't for her infernal temper. I wonder where she gets the money to dress with? I hope the usual maid doesn't make her clothes."

Mrs Normansel took the few steps which brought her from the door to Sir Hugh very slowly; then she gave him a level look, and without any spark of warmth or good humour, said, "Well?"

"Well!" cried Sir Hugh in a fuss. "Well! Upon my word, Camilla, you are not very encouraging. Here I take a long journey—and that— in the month of February—a most disagreeable journey; and on top of it I stand about—and all that—in a house as cold as a ship at sea; and you receive me—I mean—in short, you treat me as if I was the tax-collector."

"My good Hugh," replied the lady calmly, "you are very ridiculous. You never did the least thing for Richard when he was alive, or for me and the kiddies; when I asked you for help you wrote me a most abominable letter which I'll never forgive; you left me in the lurch with the children, and you didn't care, and I don't believe you knew whether I was alive or dead; and yet after all that you expect me to rush into the room and throw my arms about your neck and call you a dear old man, I suppose? It doesn't make me angry, you know. It simply bores me. That's all."

"Well, it isn't I who am angry, Camilla," said Sir Hugh. He began to be afraid that her rancour would, after all, strangle her interest, which would upset his plans; and so he fell to cry softer. "There isn't a man in England with a better temper than I have. But to come down here with my head full of notions for your benefit—and—and your children, and all that;—I don't say I haven't been a little careless, but my affairs, and my health—yes, my miserable health. But I did not, I own, expect this reception, when I have arranged—and that—everything to serve you—"

"Have you any more corners in your will?" Mrs Normansel asked significantly.

Sir Hugh fairly blushed. "I find that remark in the worst taste, Camilla," he said. "That husband of yours—he's dead now, and all that—but I'm bound to say he seems to have had a very bad effect on you. There was a man talking to me only the other night about insolence and cook-maids—very good stuff, too, very pointed—but we needn't go into that. What I came here to say, if you would give me a chance to talk—to get the words out of my mouth, so to speak—is that I am going to make you a civil offer—to put you in a mighty comfortable state, and all that;—I mean, to give you a good round income—as good, let me tell you, as my means will allow; and that strikes me—perhaps I am prejudiced—and that—but altogether, it seems to me that I do pretty well. Now what do you think?" cries Sir Hugh with some uneasiness.

"It sounds very splendid," answered Mrs Normansel in a cold voice, without conviction. "I should like to know, however, just how long it is going to last. As long as I can remember, I never knew you to keep in the same mind, where it was a matter of giving money, for six months together. It would be a pity, and really not worth while, to be hauled out of the mud to gasp for a minute or two, and then dropped back again at your caprice."

"Now that's just the thing! a very wise question!" exclaimed Sir Hugh with warmth. "You have touched it with the point—as they say, and all that. You will see how near you have come to it when I tell you—without hesitation, and all that—but to be plain, and so—what?—In short, as a matter of fact, your income shall last as long as I live—as long as I am not a denizen of the skies, as the fellow in the play says; in as few words as possible—and all that—as long as I am about the world. So the best thing you can do, Camilla, is to go down on your bare knees every day of your life and pray that I may have health and strength long—as they say, and that,—in a word, that I may last a couple of centuries."

"But after the couple of centuries," said Mrs Normansel; "what is to happen then? I'm rather curious to know how you have willed things?"

"Willed things!" cried Sir Hugh, almost in a shout, "Willed things! Why," says he, "I am very glad to tell you, Camilla, that I haven't left a single thing to anybody. No; not a bad ha'penny, not a cracked jug, not a broken chair, not an old bootlace. Nothing—no, nothing at all. That's something I want you to remember, Camilla, and you can tell it to all your friends and neighbours—and that—the louder the better."

"But that's sheer nonsense!" Mrs Normansel replied with a certain stiffness. "The estate must go to somebody after your death: it can't be melted."

"It is not nonsense," said Sir Hugh with humour, rubbing his thigh. "On the contrary, it is very plain sense. Your temper, Camilla, if you'll allow me to say so, is so little under control—I mean to say, that it blinds you. I once heard a very good sermon on bad temper, and the fellow said, after this and that—but we have no time to bother about that now. What I want to impress upon you is that the estate is out of tail, and that I can leave—in short, that I can do what I like. As a matter of fact—without any hiding or secrecy about it, but fair and plain—I can tell you that I've left one-half of my revenue to support lame dogs and horses, and the other half to the Holy Father—do you understand?—to the Pope of Rome. Neither of them, I take it—neither the horses and dogs nor the Pope—will want me to croak, and that—any sooner, because they are going to get my money. The dogs and horses *can't* know what they are coming in for, and I'll take good care the Pope *doesn't* know;—and even if he did, I'll warrant that he's the one man who wouldn't grudge another old man all the enjoyment of life he can get, merely for the sake of filling his own pockets. So that's plain,

Camilla; and now you know where you are. I make you a good, clean offer: you can get out of this hole and come to town; one of your boys can go to Eton when he's old enough, and the other you can put in the Navy or what you like; and you can have a governess for the girl. But, remember, the moment the breath is out of my body, you'll have to shift for yourself. Now let me hear what you have got to say."

Mrs Normansel paused for a moment. When she heard about the animals and the Pope it dawned upon her that her cousin's wits were moving eccentrically; but she perceived the advantage which lay in his proposal, and she thought, that let her once get a foothold, and it would go hard but she would have a hand in the business of the will. So without any wry faces she made a meal of her pride and resentment, as most women would have done in her situation, and gracefully announced to Sir Hugh that she was a subject for his bounty.

"There now—there—that's most excellent: 'pon my word you give me more joy than I ever had in my life!" cried Sir Hugh with a kind of dashed heartiness; for he was so made that to give money, even for his own interest, when he could see no immediate return, wrung him a little. "I would advise you," he continued, "to pull out of this place as soon as you can. You can have that little house of mine in Pont Street—there is no one in it now—and I'll put some furniture in for you. And now I must go: I can't stay hanging about your house, Camilla; you keep it too cold. I know it agrees with some people—and all that—to be sure, there is—fine bracing weather, and so on—but altogether it doesn't do very well—that is, it doesn't suit me—not my constitution."

"It suits the constitution of some purses," Mrs Normansel murmured. She attended him to the door, and on the threshold she made him a pretty speech.

"You know, Hugh, I think it very generous of you, most generous and kind, to come all this distance on a winter's day to make us happy. Of course we have had our quarrels, and I didn't like the way you treated poor dear Richard, and every one of the family besides; but all that is forgotten now, isn't it, and we are going to be good friends. And you may be sure, that even at the worst times, I never taught the chicks anything but good of you; and at this moment they think you are the greatest man in the world."

This was listened to with much satisfaction by Sir Hugh, who knowing himself to be lazy and unprofitable to his own family and the general humanity, was wonderfully glad to hear there were such rumours of him stirring in the mind of youth. But urged by his habitual suspicion, he disguised his complacency and only said: "I am glad you do not understand Latin, Camilla."

Mrs Normansel stared, and it occurred to her that this was a new setting of the Pope and the lame dogs. "Understand Latin?" she repeated. "How absurd you are! What on earth for?"

"Because, since that is the case," answered Sir Hugh, "I am able to ease my mind by repeating the words of the poet:—

   … Ulla putatis … Dona carere dolis Danaum? sic notus Ulixes?*

—Now, which is the way to the station?"

Chapter V

For a space of about three years (and as I hate vagueness, I will give it exact)—for two years, seven months, and three days, the peace concluded between Sir Hugh and Mrs Normansel survived and flourished: and since the times of profound peace, it is confessed, are notoriously devoided of dramatic incident, I will, if you please, take a good jump over that period, and land upon a point where the narrative once more begins to stir. But lest any one should take it upon him to insult over me for being so slack in decorum, and so loose in my methods and morals, that I abstain to linger upon the easy and God-blessed hours of peace, for the sake of pandering to those who would ever have their noses in the devil's own hell-broth of excitement—why, to avoid that, I had better give you a brief view, and as narrow as I can make it, of how matters went in the tranquil season. And here I believe there offers as good a chance as I shall ever have to protest that you are wrong if you take me for one of the lusty full-blooded fellows who are every hurrying you from post to post, and charge the intervals of road with murder, rape, and ale-house turbulence. Rather, I live so enamoured of the flat and patient aspects of the world, that if I had not to beat out a story which I must bring orderly to an end (and if I had not some kind of a story, there would be even fewer readers of this book than as it is I look for)—

* [From Virgil's, *The Aeneid*, "Do you think … any gift from the Greeks is without tricks? Is Ulysses known to you?"]

but I vow, if it were not for the story, my own genius would incline me to be here till next Sunday twelve-month twaddling about nothing. And having made that much clear, we will go back to Sir Hugh.

Never in his life had he been so well as he was at this time. His spirits were lively and serene; and from looking upon life as a pest-hole steaming forth diseases and arrayed with traps of death, he was come to regard it as a cordial garden wherein every flower he plucked revealed one more enticing. There were no more dreary spells of recruiting in the country: the passions and tastes which erewhile had laid him low, he snapped his fingers at, and indulged with impunity. His social instincts, too, under the influence of Mrs Normansel, came out of prison to assert themselves. He had taken a habit to go to the house in Pont Street four or five days in the week, and let his wit shine upon those he happened to find there. To this surprising transition he had been brought by his relish of his cousin's unresting concern for his health: the way she strangled draughts, the even temperature of her rooms, her alertness about his food, were new to him and comfortable. On her part, she supported his company with decorous composure; though not seldom after he had gone, her head would buzz for hours from his hesitating lips and windy casual sentences. But as she had not the least notion of the genuine reason for his bounty, and thought that he might at any moment in a bout of sullenness withdraw it, she fashioned herself to encounter his humours without complaint, and even with a smiling face. It seems a pity out of a million, that so dainty a state, which called for the exercise of so many virtues, should have been ruined and brought to nothingness by a dispute the most trivial you ever read of, or heard tell. You might puzzle the wits out of your noddle ere you could hit upon what this dispute was about: though I gave you to guess from now till the next full moon you would be where you were before: and if my word is not enough, and you still persist (as I should myself in such a case) that you can arrive by cogitation at the very matter—clap your hand over the rest of the page, set your eyes on the ceiling, and take five minutes of hard guessing. … Now, my dear guesser (for I protest after that little halt and personal affair between us I have warmed to you heartily) I hope you are in such a blaze of curiosity that you will weep, rave, swear, become morose, peevish, melancholy, or go violently to bed in a rage, if I don't at once tell you what actually did take place.

Chapter VI

But stay a little! Upon recollecting myself, I think it is not so well to open this matter suddenly; for it is a recognized therapeutical axiom, that sudden gratification, coming upon the top of long and vehement cravings, is a matter so periculous that hardly one in a thousand suffers it unscathed. Did not What's-his-name, after waiting for his dinner with all the uneasy appetite of a glutton, finish himself by an inordinate meal of lampreys? Have not potentates and great men, in this as well as other ages of the world, been taken off in the excitement caused by the fruition of their desires? How then, with these warnings before my eyes, can I expose you, of all people, to such a risk?—Because you must know, reader, that since you have paid the publisher the sum he asks for this volume, I feel myself bound, not only to supply you with entertainment to the best of my power, but also to look after your health, and even to coddle you a bit, as long as you remain in my hands: for in this, I take it, an author is like the manager of a play-house, who is expected not only to offer a pleasant show on the stage, but further, to keep (though precious few of them do it) all draughts, and poisonous gases, and grievous smells, from the senses of the beholders. How can I tell that you are at present in a condition to sustain a shock? How do I know that your curiosity is not at that keen edge, when to satisfy it without due preparation would be little better than a felony? How do I know you have any curiosity at all?—This last is enough to stagger my elaborate precautions: however, when all is told, what with one or two notorious instances in my head, and other things, it is wisest to go dry-shod on the safe side. Therefore, to gain time for the flames of curiosity, which may be now leaping somewhat outrageously, to reduce themselves to a calm and steady glow, I mean in this place to pursue some mild and tranquil inquiry; and the subject I propose to examine (because I particularly want to clear it up somewhere, and it seems a very act of Providence that this place should open so conveniently)— the subject is this: Wherein the sections of this Dissertation, which are by no means to be confounded with tales, differ from that form of literary exercise commonly known as a Tale. And here I would ask you (though 'tis merely a suggestion, and I am really glad to have you take your ease, so to speak, between these covers)—but I would ask you to suspend your hand, which I saw was raised at the end of the last sen-

tence to skip the rest of this chapter; for though the subject of our des-
cant may be rather staid and hodden, you cannot tell, nor can I either,
what surprises may be in store ere we have got half way through the
next paragraph.

The great Fielding, towards the end, I think, of *Tom Jones,* declares
that he could with less pains write one of the Books of his novel, than
the prefatory chapter to each of them; in like manner, I believe I could
write five long tales easier and sooner than some chapters in any section of this work. I make this confession, for one thing, that you may
see I have some respect for you as a reader, and that I do not (as I certainly might do, and remain in the fashion to boot) palm off on you
the distractions of my leisure time; and for another thing, that my
work may not be judged in a character it does not profess: whence it is
important I should announce clearly, that the sections which compose
it are not offered as tales. So (between friends), it were a waste of their
Worships' breath to rebuke me for introducing reflections, discussions,
counter-marches, and thus by digressions spoiling a story; for I never
proposed to myself when I set out, to be cribbed by the limits of a story.
No; when I do undertake a story, I may make a good hand of it, or I
may not; but you may safely take an oath on the heads of your ancestors
that it will be wholly unlike anything this book contains. By the foot
of Pharaoh! how it braces and tonifies me amidst these serious labours
when I think of the story I mean to write. It will be to no purpose
for indignant champions of true literature to prate me at that inspired
moment about curbing my unruly pen. You, grave sirs, may call after
me then your reproaches till your thrapples crack: I'll toss them back
in your beards. Then shall I revel in the unholy, and give nervous hours
to the guardians of the Young Miss; then shall the odour of what used
to be called in the olden time, Decadence, linger like the faint perfume
of a dead flower upon every page. ... But as for this discreet work, let
me reassure honourable and right honourable gentlemen that I have at
present far other business in my head than the making of stories. All
that I endeavour (if I can claim to endeavour anything) is to show the
events which arise in four cases when two beings, essentially different
in character and most things else, are thrown together by a fatal accident; by which expression I would be understood to mean, the rage and
mockery of the Fates. See, they float together a space with the futility
of two snow-flakes on a winter's gale; then one gets the worst of it, con-

sciously or not does the work of the other, and goes under. This is my theme; and though you may observe as we get on, I am often enticed from it to pursue strange visions across the hills which unexpectedly spring up by the roadside—a vagrom habit I am gratifying here and now in this chapter; still, you will discover that to this theme, from these Venusbergs, I always return pensively, a chastened palmer, in the end. Now I have already said, and care not if I repeat it, that the sections wherein this theme is developed are not separate tales, but rather blended and correlated so inextricably that they make one piece, "as a good house-wife (says he) out of divers fleeces weaves one piece of cloth." From this I am encouraged to advance the request which, in effect, is the true aim of this excursion: That you will consider of these intentions of mine, ere you bring me in guilty of making a mess of a business I was never upon. Nay, though you find me before many chapters are passed going over some heavy ground rather sportingly,— which indeed I think extremely probable, for I'll not answer for it that I shall be able to keep up a doctrinal solemn tone, like this I employ here, through some hundreds of pages containing the most various and extraordinary matters; yet that lighter method of getting across country, d'ye mark, will not be indulged by way of telling a tale seriously, but rather of rounding a truth agreeably. Surely, my notions of a tale are very strict and exact. In the first place you must—But enough, enough! 'Tis merciless; I scorn to do it!

For, to say the truth, this begins to sound disagreeably like a Preface; and now-a-days a preface is in a book, very much what a sermon is in the life of the world. There is nothing I dread more than the look which would overspread your face were you to meet a preface stalking in this place, where it would be about as apposite as a sermon at a masqued ball; a discursus on the Epistles of St Paul at the opera; a—a—what shall I say?—a lecture on the use of the globes at a wedding. Lord ha' mercy, I am choused, cozened, betrayed! you would cry; and with all the more reason because you thought you had fortunately escaped the Preface when you looked for it, at the beginning of the book. But fear not; you are as safe from prefaces here as you are from prayers: and since I know as well as any one, there is nothing more injurious than to inhale for long the tainted and mephitical atmosphere of any weighty explanations or theories, we will this minute change into another room, where (now that your blood is cool and your pulse orderly) we may reveal without danger the secret which was left trembling in the air at the end of the last chapter.

Chapter VII

It happened one afternoon when Sir Hugh, according to his custom, was drinking tea with his cousin, that they had the room to themselves. I have said they were drinking tea; but I would like to make a little change, whereof you will see the importance by-and-bye, and say, rather, that while Mrs Normansel was drinking tea, Sir Hugh was drinking coffee.

"Tea comes just at the right hour," Mrs Normansel remarked inanely; for she was tired and bored.

Sir Hugh was neither the one nor the other. "I wonder, Camilla, that you can make so unreflecting an observation," he replied with great sprightliness. "If you'll only allow yourself to think—and all that—you must remember that you have heard me scores of times—of course I'm not a doctor—and that—but I've gone into these matters;—and I'm sure you've heard me say at least fifty times—quite fifty—perhaps more—perhaps more—that tea taken in the evening is poison—no less. The only time to take tea—I'm well up in these things—is the early morning."

They had often discussed this subject before (indeed, by this time, it would have been difficult to hit upon any subject within Sir Hugh's range which they had not discussed before), and it was usual for Mrs Normansel, whenever it began to look like an argument, to let her opinion go by the board. But to-day from some cause she had a fit of the spleen, and her nerves were not under complete control; and, moreover, this was a question which she always found it most difficult to be passive about, as she plumed herself on her medical knowledge. So she answered somewhat impatiently:

"My dear Hugh, that is one of your ridiculous fads. All the world knows that tea in the afternoon is exhilarating and pulls you together; while in the morning, on the contrary, it is really injurious. I never touch it in the morning."

"You may call it a fad, or what you like," says Sir Hugh, very ruffled. "I don't know about all the World—unless they are fools—and all that—but I own it strikes me, when I tell you I've made researches—

and so on—that you might pay a little more—in short, you ought to see that I'm right."

Here the matter was allowed for the moment to stand; and the two talked for a while in guarded terms about things not in controversy. But though their minds worked in distinct ways, still they turned on the same subject; and two pairs of compasses, given the same centre and an equal radius, though twisted in opposite directions, must at some point of the circle infallibly collide. So it came about that Mrs Normansel at last, either by accident or design, and let us hope it was the former (though I am not so sure), said to Sir Hugh: "Will you have some more tea?"

"Tea!" cried Sir Hugh, now thoroughly vexed. "Tea! Upon my word, Camilla, you are enough to provoke bad language from a nun. Here am I—quiet, and all that—and souse you go into that scandalous subject again. This habit you have of bursting out—I mean, your conversation always smacks of the bosom of the family. I hope you don't make a practice of talking to every one as if you were in the bosom of your family. Really, with your dreadful temper—never forgiving injuries—and all that—quite savage, I declare! I explain to you about poison—and that—hit it off very well—in short, just to the point—and upon my word you—you laugh in my face!"

"My good Hugh," replied the lady with maddening placidity, "how odd of you! Why is it that you can't see what everybody else sees? Everybody knows that tea is harmful after a long fast. You take it in the morning, and you do a great many other things that are bad for you; but you have survived what would kill a regiment;—not one man in fifty thousand has your luck. The sure proof that tea in the morn-ing is poison, is that you think it poison in the afternoon. Tea in the morning has destroyed thousands, and" (quoth Mrs Normansel with a laugh) "apparently it makes me sin against the light. If I'm not careful, it will land me in the Home for the Indigent Blind. I always read that Indignant Blind, don't you?"

"I see nothing to laugh at," Sir Hugh retorted (for it had come to that) in a great passion. "I take leave to say—in fact, I consider you indecent. I never was so disgusted—never, upon my life—quite out of the com-mon. I have the honour—and that—to wish you good-afternoon. I felt to be here—it may be, perhaps—perpetual rush—come and go—enter-taining and all that;—but I own there was something—what with your temper—and the rest—that didn't exactly please me;—knew it couldn't last, and in fact I said so. Good afternoon," he said again from the door. "That poor creature your husband—I confess I didn't know what he had to endure—scenes, and that, scenes—I never liked him—always thought him a fool. But I'll tell you plainly—without any nonsense— that I prefer a fool to a—to a—not to mince matters—well—a shrew! Good afternoon!" And on that word he took himself away.

As he drove to his club his rage increased, and he determined to have done with Mrs Normansel once for all. Dull with fury, he flung the suggestions of prudence out of his head; and this he did without compunction, since from having long gone scatheless, he had waxed reckless in ill-living. Therefore, when he got to his club, he composed this letter:—

> "My dear Camilla,—Upon a calm and unprejudiced consideration of your extraordinary conduct this afternoon, I am convinced that it will be happier and easier for both of us if we have no further intercourse. I have therefore instructed my solicitor that whatever benefits you draw at present from my estate, are to cease. I cannot conclude without offering you a word of friendly advice to manage your really dangerous temper, which, if you don't, will some day place you in a situation affected by the criminal law.—Yours very sincerely,
>
> HUGH WROTHSLEY ANGER."

As his rage would not let him stay his revenge, he sent this letter by a messenger, and told him to wait for an answer; but it was by the post he got the following reply:—

> "Dear Hugh,—Your letter has given me more pain than ever I had in my life, and it is all so unfair too. When I first read it I felt like crying my eyes out, that I and the children should have to depend on so cruel a wretch. But I have got over that now; and as I shall probably marry, your assistance may not be missed so much as you hope it will. As for my temper, in future I will take the best means possible to mend that, by trying to imitate yours.—Ever,
>
> CAMILLA NORMANSEL.
>
> "P.S.—I met Sir Joseph Baxter (M.D., F.R.S., and goodness knows what else), last night, and he *quite* agrees with me that tea is bad in the morning. Perhaps his opinion will convince you, if poor mine can't."

You have never seen a letter which you have used for a light, put a fire to any substance combustible quicker than the above letter started Sir Hugh's smouldering wrath into a blaze. "Sir Joseph Baxter!" he sputtered, "Sir Joseph Baxter! What more does he know about tea-drinking than I do? I would stand out the whole college of 'em in a matter that I've gone into myself." And filled with a rollicking intoxication by this defiance of his old masters, the physicians, he issued into the night of rain and fog, and did not seek his own bed till his servants were leaving theirs.

Chapter VIII

But alack! the triumph, although specious and vehement, did not endure—no, not twenty-four hours. Sir Hugh awoke after his debauch in a most dismal state, agonized and impotent: and thenceforward for three weeks he lay on his couch, a shattered, fearful old man, surrounded by doctors and nurses, who looked every moment to see him expire. But by a miracle which set the doctors by the ears, and which, for what I know, they are still discussing, he managed to keep the soul in his body: and as soon as he was enough recovered to realize the danger he had passed, and to dread a like disaster, he searched among his papers for the German's address; and then, with trembling legs, and wits—still mothery, he made a journey to the university town of Göttingen.

He found his counsellor in a clear spacious room, seated on the floor, employed in the edification of castles with children's bricks. Sir Hugh whose mind was full of histories of life and death, was violently shocked by the insouciant and nursery character of this pastime; but he was quickly reassured when his host got to his feet without manifesting the least surprise at the visit, and at once assumed those brave airs of authority, steadiness, and freedom from doubt which had fascinated him at first.

"It is Seneca who observes," said the German, noting that Sir Hugh kept his eye upon the bricks, "that children's employments and delights differ in impertinency from the greatest, of the greatest part of men, only in degrees. But I perceive that at this moment the toy you prefer is yourself, and so let us look to your working. I gather," he went on, lighting a pipe of tobacco, "I gather from your low look and shaking limbs that you have neglected my instructions."

"My dear sir," replied Sir Hugh in a piping voice, "I've been nearer the black hole—and that—than I'll ever be till I tumble in. Ill? I should think—what with doctors and all that—quite what you call the nursing party—fact—fact I assure you. But I was extremely indisposed indeed—my nerves and all that—my system had quite—And the whole thing was—after attentions and things of that sort—if you follow me,—dancing at her petticoats—rushing about for her pleasure day and night—never getting a wink to myself, as much out of bed as in—at my age, d'ye see, at my age—a she-cousin of mine, if you please—no one better—one of my miserable relations, as you understand, became—in short, turned out to be a perfect wild cat." And he proceeded to relate the circumstances which had led to the difference between Mrs Normansel and himself.

The other heard him to the end without interruption, and then observed tranquilly:

"I suppose you could not bring yourself to think after the fashion of those philosophers who hold that when the soul is expelled from the body it mingles with the air; and hence it comes that men more spiritual and ascetic than the common can often hear the laugh of souls in the wind. You might find sufficient pleasure in such a thought to combat your terror of death. For surely after we have cast this troubled body, it can be no sombre destiny to dwell within the winds which carry the eternal voice from the high stars to flowers in a neglected garden, or to a piece of sea-weed floating on a dark sea, and so give them part in the commotion of the universe."

"Very good—and all that," quoth Sir Hugh. "Very excellent—quite out of the ordinary—and the rest of it; but a little what we call—eh?—In fact, it strikes me—I may be wrong,—and so—but I own, I feel safer where I am. I'm a great man for sticking where I find myself. Of course there's philosophy, and that—very deep studies;—but we waste a vast deal of time over this and the other—quite unsettling. Why, there was a chap in the Service when I was a lad took to philosophy and things of that sort,—always talking about the will to do this and the will to do that;—and begad! if five months after he didn't marry a circus rider. Ugliest little French beast you ever saw. It's wonderful what strength people get from these studies—strength of mind, and so on. And I hope you will give me leave to tell you, sir," says Sir Hugh, "that your own country seems to have an odd effect on your wits. Bless my life!—you are quite poetized,—stars and flowers and the rest of it. Now, when I saw you in England—you must take it as you like, but, indeed, there was no poetry about you then."

"That is most probable," responded the other, passing his hand across his brow. "The effect of the breath of a multitude of people on the mind of a man is a matter to be noted. Surely, when I am inhaling the air which millions of Englishmen are breathing, my mind and spirits must be different from what they are when I am breathing the air with Germans or Austrians. Again; when you go to France or Italy, your spirits are more impulsive, and your mind more active and brilliant, but less sedate and orderly; and this, not so much (as it is loosely and commonly held) because of the climate, and a clearer sky, but because you are respiring the breath of a Latin race. Further, in great cities you are ever breathing in everybody else's sins, and vices, and sorrows; and that is why after a long sojourn in a city, there comes a certain faintness and droop of the spirits, and with some a disposition to crime. Wherefore, after dwelling for many months in a city, it is well to repair to some thinly inhabited neighbourhood, where the people have neat and simple thoughts, that the mind may be cleansed, and filled with those elements which bring us peace.

"I am at present engaged," pursued the German, "in developing a somewhat curious and subtle theory of the power of certain words. For I hold that words and brief phrases such as *Yes*, *No*, *Stand still*, *Lie down*, have acquired, from being used daily by multitudes, a force inherent to themselves (I do not at all mean, as I will explain at length in a minute, their power to indicate the human will)—but such words have a force in themselves which is lacking, say, in the less used terminology of the metaphysics. Now, if you will examine with any care—But I see," remarked the gentleman, "that you are somewhat impatient."

"Not at all," said Sir Hugh, shuffling his feet; "not at all. Very glad to have the benefit—and all that. But when you come to think I've travelled over hill and dale, so to speak—wretched German trains, and the rest—hanging about—fingering, you know, fingering—well, you must forgive me, but I should like to hear about my own subject. Perhaps another time, over the—and so on, as the song says—I say, all being well, we may go into—But at present I'm bound to say it strikes me,— and besides—I hope you will pardon me—but there doesn't seem about you that air of laying down the law, that certain knowledge, so to speak, which impressed me before—took the wind out of my sails—and all that. There is, to be sure, in your manner—but your words, sir, your words—"

"You are right: I am not so sure as I was three years ago," answered the other, without any show of annoyance at this tirade. "You have, to a certain degree, spoiled, or at least altered the game, and that is why I delay to consider new moves in it. However, there is now only one thing left for you to do, and that is, to go back to your cousin. She has more will-power, a stronger love of riches and a stronger hate, than all the rest of your pensioners put together. Her will enabled you to live with ease and even enjoyment during the last three years: when it was withdrawn, became indifferent, or, it may be, even active for your death, you were carried to the brink of the grave, and the combined wills of your other pensioners were only just strong enough to prevent you from going down."

"Them I have, at any rate, thank God!" cried Sir Hugh in a burst of fervour; for he was aghast at the thought of surrendering his arms to the triumphant sound of the drums and trumpets of Mrs Normansel; in other words, of giving up his darling contention beneath her satirical and indulgent smiles.

"Yes, you have them," assented the other. "But what are so many against the one, after all? If one of them were to die to-morrow, and thus weaken the corporation of will in your favour while Mrs Normansel remained hostile, you might give up hope—that would be the end. And think not to stay your perplexity by adding new pensioners to the old; for the force of wills increase in direct *ratio* to the length of time they have been exerted. Besides, your cousin, Mrs Normansel, is an exception. I am not unwilling to confess, that when I put you upon this business I did not contemplate the entrance into your life of a single character so strong, with so many influences upon you, and such a command of your weaknesses. I am not blind to her errors. I feel she is a clever woman, and yet she has been stupid enough to treat you as a fool. Now, my dear sir, my greatly honoured disciple, let me conjure you never to treat the greatest dolt and wooden dunce who stumbles across your path as a fool. Not the feculent parliamentarian, whose turbid soul stares with a dull vacuity of eye while he repeats to you the phrases he has caught from the front bench; not the sot who holds an office which is only more important than himself, and upon that gives himself the airs of a dispenser of kingdoms; not the deplorable ass who will instruct soldiers in military tactics, sailors in the navigation of the sea, and all men in the arts which they have studied and he has heard of"—

["That's Camilla," quoth Sir Hugh];—"nor he who is so awry as to the respect which others bear him, that he takes heavy airs of patronage, and gives of his emptiness with a condescending smile; nor the fatuous yet pathetic mother who believes, and protests on all occasions to all comers, that her commonplace children are Goethes, Leonardos, and Mozarts; nor (perhaps worst of all) the poor, weak ninny who looks satisfied with the world, and with his stupid and pretentious smirk of invitation, conquering eyes, and the overdone momentary distinction of a tailor's plate, imagines (and they give him reason) that by his graces he bewitches and enchants all the women whom he cares to attract;—no, never scorn them for fools, but rather to all these I implore you, sir, to extend your fashions of civility; for if you be wise, a wise man may perceive your wisdom, but a fool never will: and therefore it is—"

"Fools—fools all," interrupted Sir Hugh, setting up a laugh. "Quite what you may call a constellation. I know them—every one of them;—I've met the lot of 'em in my time—in one way or other—back and front. Why, there was the wife of old Trumbull—I could tell you a good story about that. You must remind me. Ha, ha, ha! I'll bet a sovereign it was all a pack of lies. But, Lord! at seven o'clock in the morning!—My way with these people is to take them mildly, but firmly—firmly, you know, and all that—the iron hand eh?—let them see I won't stand their damned nonsense—and all the rest of it."

"But as for your cousin," resumed the German, "the mistake she made, as I have said, was to treat you like a fool. She will not do that again: she will either go up or down: though I acknowledge that precisely how she will act is beyond my conjecture. But if you wish to go on living you must once more get her will on your side. With that in your favour, you shall be carried triumphantly through the years. When she grows old and weak and her will for good and evil is numbing, you can form a new body of pensioners and make a mockery of her dissolution. Sir, you may see the rise and destruction of what men call lasting kingdoms, and the adventures of a life may come to be for you as the passing incidents of a day.—You find me uncertain," he added, taking Sir Hugh by the hand, "uncertain and perhaps fantastical; but there is one thing I can assert with confidence, which is, that your liberation rests within yourself." And as he thus spoke he smiled the same mirthless smile which before had fallen upon Sir Hugh in the library at night.

Chapter IX

Sir Hugh returned to England; and after some parleys, and the service
of a Mrs Ardour (a celebrated woman whom Sir Hugh hated, but who
was a great friend of Mrs Normansel) and other ambassadors, the relations between him and his cousin being redintegrate, he began to lead
a new life. For there had now come to Mrs Normansel a knowledge of
her power: she had studied Sir Hugh too closely not to know that he
would never have sunk his quarrel if he had not been driven to it by
some motive of self-interest: and knowing her power, she abased it to a
flagrant and merciless despotism. Sir Hugh, pour soul! became a mere
feather before her whims. The German was right in so far as she treated
him no longer as a fool; but she treated him as a slave, which is on all-
fours with the other, unless it be worse. His tastes and humours were
no longer noted and managed; his stories and opinions were no longer
related to a face of patience; and all that was left of the former situation
was the sedulous care of his health. This waxed into something gigantic, feverish, abnormal. Every morsel Sir Hugh put into his mouth, all
the motions of his body, were arranged and recorded; and it became
for him an affair of out-posts to escape from his cousin's scrutiny. As
she had taken of late a passion for travelling, she dragged in the wake
of her family the unhappy old man who loathed every country save
England, hither and thither, in maddening flights across Europe: to
Egypt one winter, to Algiers another;—and not, you will believe, from
any love of his company, but because she thought he might injure his
health if he was beyond her inspection. As for money, be sure she was
not contented with the allowance of an earlier time, but now explored
all the avenues of extravagance; lavished on herself, lavished on her
children, poured money out of windows and doors, in the frenzy of a
woman who after a long restraint, has at last given a loose to her passion. If Sir Hugh ventured to protest against this disorganization and
corruption of his estate, he was struck dumb by an offer on her part
to abandon the camp, and retire with her children to a cottage in the
country; and at the simple mention of this the sweat sprang on him like
a shower: for though, in sooth, he enjoyed not at all his present game
of life, his disgust was but a vapour when weighed against his hatred
of death. In sum, I can think of nothing so pat to make you realize his
situation, as to compare it to that of an infatuated old man who knows

that he is being ruined, outraged, and betrayed day after day by a young and pretty mistress; and yet will cling on for the sake of the crusts. But I feel, sir, that a man of your acuteness and knowledge of the world will not delay to observe, that a crust, even, is some reward; and if a man likes to pay heavily for leave to beg for crusts, who are we to gainsay him?—I agree with all that to the last word; you cannot advance anything which jumps better with my own humour: and what made Sir Hugh's case the harder was that he had not the ghost of a crust to exercise his teeth upon, unless it were the virtuous thoughts which are said to arise from effusive charity. For Mrs Normansel was no longer very pretty or very young, and I hasten to say (for I'll have no bawdry in my book) that even if she had been, Sir Hugh might have gone down on his marrow-bones to her for a year and a day, and found at the end, that for all he had gained of her favour, he might have spent the time in digging potatoes.

But the one point wherefrom Sir Hugh could not be moved by all the arts and entreaties, wiles and storms that ever carried riot into a private family, was the construction of his will. No; the money ("what is left of it," he would say with a sigh), must go after his death to lame dogs and horses, and the Pope. 'Twas in vain for Mrs Normansel, who was ignorant of the reasons which gave him resolution, to deplore his senile obstinacy: sooner than move him, she could have lifted a horse in her arms. And to this great rebuff, there was added the slighter vexation of the other pensioners, whom, in her continual busying about Sir Hugh's money, she had discovered. She set her face hard against what she termed her cousin's ridiculous and criminal philanthropy; and but for the iron letter of the law which she could not abrade, the pensioners, good honest creatures! would have had the bread of idleness torn from their mouths. But years passed, and one by one the pensioners dropped beyond all human bounty or malice; and Sir Hugh, who had learned from the German how useless they were to him when opposed to Mrs Normansel, watched them go without a pang.

The death of the last dependant was not without an effect. One day when Sir Hugh, having escaped by chance from his monitor, was spending an easy hour at his club, his kinsman, Shawlcoat Vellery, who had *The Times* in his hand, looked up and said:

"I see that man in the Indian Civil whom Camilla says you were so good to, has just died at Madras," and he held out the paper.

Sir Hugh read the notice with sour deliberation; and although he had never much rested upon the pensioners, he thought grimly that now, more than ever, it was Camilla or the deeps.

"I have always supposed," observed Mr Vellery, using the terms of assertion, though his tone was pitched to a question, "that all your money will ultimately go to Camilla and her children."

"Oh, Camilla—there is no one but Camilla," quoth Sir Hugh absently, with a vague gesture.

Taking this for an assent, Mr Vellery, when a few days afterward he was alone with Mrs Normansel, mentioned it as a fact well known that she was to inherit Sir Hugh's fortune.

The lady's brows started up. "Not a bit of it," she cried quickly; "it's nothing at all like that. The ridiculous old miscreant," said she, with a little fleck of temper on her cheeks, "has left everything to a home for lame cats or dogs;—I never could remember which, and I don't think I ever had the patience to find out."

"All I can say," replied Mr Vellery, "is that I had it from himself. We were talking the other day about family matters, and I ventured, as his kinsman, to ask him, in so many words, if he had left the estate to you, and he answered, in so many words, that he had."

Thereupon a wave of light rolled across the mind of Mrs Normansel. Like the rest of the world, she attributed to Sir Hugh a kind heart, an ornament which she had always considered with regret and contempt; but now she began to see, that it might (in another) be a possession of genuine practical value. For the story of the dogs and horses struck her, of a sudden, as an obvious clumsy jape, and matter for noon-tide laughter: she smoked in it a scheme, born from the oddity of Sir Hugh, to cast a veil over his active intentions of benevolence towards herself and her children; and from that moment there was an end of her hesitation to credit the report of Mr Vellery.

At this place I must make a new paragraph, to emphasize the importance of what is now to be related.

When, with the common propensity of men and women to deceive themselves concerning the affection which they are held in by others (for if she had thought clearly, she must have perceived that Sir Hugh, although he allowed her to spend his money, had never shown that he loved her, and indeed, had not much reason to love her or her retinue)—when Mrs Normansel, I say, became convinced that the galleons of her cousin were consigned to her wharves; as himself and his personal qualities she valued not a rush, she fell to wishing for his death with more vigour and heartiness than she had ever wished for his life.

So it came about, that Sir Hugh, from the condition of a portly gentleman whose blood ran in a warm tide and high, and who, as the phrase goes, "didn't look half his years," within a week fell incredibly aged, toothless, and decrepit; and leaving to struggle, took to his bed for the last time in the world.

And here, at a point where, according to the rubric, my narrative should be brisk, I venture, nevertheless, a delay for the sake of observing, that to follow the career of a hero to the very grave, while there is some good to be said of it, is yet, on the whole, but a barbarous and mournful business. For let your hero be in no matter how tight a place, if you leave him while the breath is still in his body, you may hope against hope to meet him once more with a smiling face, and embark upon the merriest adventure; but, on the other side, once acknowledge he is dead, and that you have seen the funeral candles, and I'll be shot if it is not for all the world like a champagne gone flat. Though the same wine is there, the smack and sparkle are not; and though you have the prettiest most moving story up your sleeve to relate of your hero, you will do better to leave it untold—you will make no good hand of it: because the imagination which, if the hero were alive, would be ever springing from the thought of what he is doing to the thought of what he will do, now stumbles contristed and leaden, pierced by the certainty that whatever he did has been struck to ashes, since he is dead.

I have thought it as well to have this matter clear with the reader, so that he may be prepared to part with Sir Hugh in the next pages; for other adventures wherein Sir Hugh cut a figure, such as—

> The tale of Sir Hugh, his neighbour Thorcanby, and the east wind;
> The tale of Sir Hugh, old Trumbull's wife, and the small hours;

—these and other conceits which at one time I intended to follow up, I now consider, form the foregoing reasons, had better remain in shadow.

⤶

Mrs Normansel watched by the couch of Sir Hugh with unfailing concern, and when she saw the end was not far off, she poured into his ears a canticle of gratitude.

"You have been so good to us, Hugh!" she cried with many tears, in a sudden rush of affection which I'll wager was genuine. "How can we ever forget you! You have done all you could—educated the children, taken us on long voyages, and lots of other things, all out of your love and good-feeling for your own people. I could break my heart to think it is over, and that you have heaped up all your kindnesses by leaving the estate to me;"—and she took his hand and kissed it; I swear to you she did.

Sir Hugh stirred a little. "How—what estate?" he asked, opening his tired old eyes.

"Your own estate, Hugh dear," softly replied Mrs Normansel, who thought he did not follow what she said. "Your estate, which you have settled in the family."

"My estate?" repeated Sir Hugh, low and wearily. "How on earth did you get that into your head? If I've told you once, I've told you ten thousand times,—I'm near my death now—and all that—and I mind what I'm saying;—but I've tried to get it into your head that everything of mine goes to the animals and the Pope."

"Do you mean to say you have stuck to that?" cried Mrs Normansel in a passion of fear. She turned pale; and then a hot flush came to her cheeks and burned away her tears. "Why, Shawlcoat Vellery said that you told him you had left all the property to me."

I regret that Sir Hugh disordered the solemnity of his death-bed by a word of comedy. "Done, by the Lord!" said he, and chuckled till the mirth rattled in his throat. "Listen to me, Camilla," said Sir Hugh. "I've come to the end of my life—I'm spun out, and nothing can save me. I'm touching death at this minute; and now that I see how soft it is, I think I was a fool to swallow all the bother and misery in life to avoid it. I'm glad about Shawlcoat's mistake, because it has set me free: I wouldn't say that if I thought you could call me back—but you can't—no, nor any one: I'm too far gone, thank God!—too far gone."

As he spoke these words he began to draw his speech at length. "Camilla," he added in a whisper with a failing tongue, "neither you nor one of my relations shall touch—"

And thereupon, whether it was from the exertion of speaking, or (as the doctors said) from a failure of the heart, or (as I say) from the thought of his relations, certain it is, that leaving his cousin to her consternation, he incontinent departed this life.

And that I may have nothing unfinished, let me add, that Mrs Normansel intends to institute a suit at law against the Holy Father.

𝓬

Section II

OF ACCOMPLICES

Chapter I

M R SHAWLCOAT VELLERY, THE KINSMAN of Sir Hugh Anger, could not remember the time when he did not wish to be a villain. His instincts had their root in hell; his emotions were stirred and set a-going by the devil; and it was his wont to sit for hours in a gay devising of iniquities. Withal, he was a man of a jovial formosity of countenance, not unlike a churchman's; and he had a frank eye and nimble merry tongue which made him agreeable to the staid and fastidious people by whom, more through his fate than his will, he was surrounded. He was a tall man, well built, who loved to shoot, to hunt the fox, and the smell of the field. His virtues, you will be surprised to hear on top of the first sentence, were used to adorn many a domestic homily.

For, in sooth, with all his study, he was but a parody of your lusty and hot-bellied sinner. He had all the will in the world; but his flesh, poor gentleman! was weak. He seemed, in effect, to live under a spell which limited his peccancy to desire, and lent to his actions the pallid aspect of decorum. Thus, he would at times be wholly given up to venereal fantasies, and thereupon choose out some comely fresh creature to debauch, and lay his traps with the ingenuity of a veteran rakehell: but when it came to the work, Lord! what a mess he would make of it between his timidity and awkward phrases, and the cold manner which settled on him at such moments, so that he would be fain at last to abandon the field in disorder, with the damsel's laughter (and contempt, too, I wot) stinging him like an arrow. Again, he would frequent stews, and gambling-dens, and the like crapulous places which are hid in cities; but ere long he discovered to his grief that he was unable to enter with any gusto into the pleasures of those he found therein, and by consequence was regarded with a sullen eye. He had, unhappily, an air a little formal and refined which he could not for the life of him put off: hereditary rags of honour fluttered about him, and though his mind rebelled, he could not help showing a physical disgust at what he saw. His ingenuous countenance shed a damp upon a genial and criminal society; and the captains and high priestesses of those tabernacles of robbers soon offered a rough shoulder to one who had a manner as little flexible and accommodating as a Fellow of a College. As disheartening a failure was the result of his dealing with other vices. His head would not allow him to be a drunkard, nor his stomach to be a glutton; he was too rich to be covetous, and his sanguine full spirits kept him from sloth; of ambition, or any tickling desire to get ahead of his fellows he had not a sign, and therefore no crabbed envy; and he had the kindest, sweetest, most obliging temper in the kingdom. As for pride and vain-glory, how could he strut and flourish it under the sun, when he had miserably failed in the one business he had set out upon—to be a notorious sinner. "What a fate is mine!" he would cry, when from thinking over his good deeds he started a vein of melancholy; "what a fate is mine, that I (of all men) should have appointed to me as Angel Guardian the mightiest wrestler before the Lord in all Paradise. With the angels of other men the Devil, in his tussles, not seldom wins a fall; but he never dares even to raise his hand to mine. Night is to my angel the same as day; sleeping as waking; he vexes the soul out of me with his eternal presence as the prudent and guarding friend; never for forty odd years has he left me one moment to myself; I might as well endeavour to fly from here to Jerusalem as to escape his intolerable vigilance. Other men's angels are sentinels who give an alarum, or pleaders who set forth their opinions, and there's an end on't: mine is simply a policeman. Alas!" Mr Vellery would sigh, and wring his hands, "I greatly fear that I shall go down to my grave as the man who could not sin."

Chapter II

I protest, that if I have a weakness for one way more than another to tell a story, 'tis for the way I am following in this,—which is, to set forth the opinions and principles of my hero in the first chapter, and then in the second chapter, to raise up an incident that will show how his opinions and principles stand the weather. And let me hasten, my very good Lord, most reverend and esteemed Sir, and my dainty Madam, to wipe out the frown which I see gathering on your brows, and to still your words of reproof, by declaring that I know, as well as you can tell me, I have no business to be giving my notions of writing a story at this stage of the performance. And doubtless what you say is true, that Balzac, and Edgar Allan Poe, and Barber d'Aurevilly, and des Periers, and Diggory Where, Boufflers, Voltaire, and Colonel Blood, together with other masters of narrative or exegesis, would gravely disapprove (but again, there is a chance they might not) of the intrusion of unrelated matter before we have got into clear water. Be that as it will, I must now say (for I shall never be easy till I've said it), that my sole poor pride and happiness in this book is that in every section it contains I have broken the canons of Art at least twice, and in two or three of them, I am sure, a great many times more.

Come, let us now rejoin Mr Shawlcoat Vellery, as he steps forth from the house of Mrs Normansel, where he has been dining on a warm evening in June. He walked slowly down Pont Street, and as the night was fine and suggested sauntering, he strolled without any direction through the streets in a great serenity of mind. He had thus proceeded for better than half-an-hour, when he found himself pacing a somewhat dark street of residences in Kensington, Smoking a cigar, looking idly about, and letting each foot he put to the ground tarry a breath ere he raised it again, so he was advancing, when a man came round a corner at a brisk walk and took the road in front of him. The man had not yet gone many steps when the door of a house, sharply thrown wide, shot a stripe of light across the causeway, and a young fellow in a drunken and bewildered condition stood simpering for a moment on the threshold, and then, as the door was slammed at his back, he wavered forward and fell with a gurgling laugh into the arms of the passenger. But this one, far from receiving the advance in an easy spirit of frolic, took a grip of the relaxed young man, and spurned him off with such force, that the head of the unhappy reveller struck with a thwack in the gutter. This done, the man spat with evident rancour at the prostrate figure, and moved on at a mended gait, making as he went certain mystical gestures with his right hand. Mr Vellery, when he saw him after voiding his spittle on his victim carelessly depart, and as he continued down the street, describe circles with his outstretched forefinger, or, anon, raise his hand to the level of his cheek and open and shut it many times in quick succession, was filled with horror; and yielding without thought to his impulse, he ran to assist the helpless creature in the kennel, and cried lustily for help. His cries, before long, attracted a few people to the silent, respectable street, and amongst them was a policeman, to whom Mr Vellery was in the act of entrusting the senseless body, when a window on the third floor of the house where-from the young man had been expelled, was suddenly flung open, and a young lady, of manifest great beauty, thrust out her head and incontinently fell into a passion of weeping. The policeman looked up; the young lady cried something inarticulate and waved her handkerchief: a man of aged reverend figure, carrying a light, appeared behind the young lady—

"All this is not my business," quoth Mr Vellery to himself; and he resumed his interrupted stroll.

Chapter III

As he walked, he began to muse and commune with himself that he had within the last quarter of an hour, effectually gainsaid his principles and closest wishes for the ordering of his life. Here he had just witnessed a magnificent sin, and act of Pagan cruelty; and instead of standing to admire, or endeavouring, as far as his weak nature would permit, to imitate it, he must, if you please, rush to the assistance of the stricken, and cry out indignantly upon the sinner. "It's useless to struggle," he murmured in profound dejection; "my wretched impulses are ever my ruin. I cannot see a brave rousing sin, but I must be for trying to get it undone. What baseness! what cowardice!" Sad and discouraged, be turned into a well-lit, busy square, and paused to light a cigarette: but his bitter meditations had taken away any relish for tobacco, and as he cast the cigarette from him with impatient disgust, it struck against a man who was reading a parish notice by the advantage of a street lamp. He turned to apologize; and then inspecting the man with keener attention, he recognized him for the very sinner who occupied his thoughts.

The man addressed him with a placid yet churlish civility. "I saw you trying to help that scum down there," he said with a toss of the head; "but let me tell you, all that is a waste of time—mere rubbish. We have enough to do in this world to fight the beasts who surround us, without reviving the ones who are knocked out. If you see a man dying, let him die. Every man has all men against him: why do you want to add another to the number? It amazes me that at your age you have not perceived these things!"

Mr Vellery was a little stung by this last sally, for he prided himself upon being a young and well-wearing man; and his friends were in a conspiracy to encourage his belief. But he was so intrigued by the flavour of sin which the stranger gave forth, that he put the affront aside, as he reviewed the speaker with a closer scrutiny. This one had a face pale and somewhat tabid, which was partly hid by a near-bitten pointed beard. He wore a loose black coat with a cape to it; and a piece of black cloth twisted round his neck and knotted, served him for collar and tie. His long black hair was covered by a soft hat with a wide brim, and he carried a thorn stick under his arm. There was in his accent, more than in his speech, signs that he had spent a good part of his life in a mean sort of company; and he would sometimes come out, Mr Vellery found, with the strident phrases, and the positive hammer-and-anvil mode of assertion affected by half-educated, or, what is often much the same, self-educated social agitators, and others of the like nature. But it needed a far more serious offence in the man than a trick of scanning every syllable of his words as though he were not used to them, to make Mr Vellery forego the pleasure which be promised himself from a conversation with one whose face was lined and set with the marks of many passions. Therefore, "You interest me prodigiously," he said in a cordial tone. "Nothing could give me more pleasure than to be acquainted with your history."

The stranger smiled at this eagerness, yet with something sombre and jeering in his look. "You remind me," he said, "of the fashion of the eighteenth century novel, where, if I remember right, the hero is constantly falling in with adventurers whom he invites, without any certain prospect of entertainment, to relate their exploits. But as it happens," he continued, "nothing in the world is easier and more pleasant than to satisfy you in this case, since (to put it nakedly) there is but one subject which I never tire to discourse upon, and that subject is Myself. Besides, owing to ungrateful circumstances, I have more idle hours on my hands than I willingly think of; and this is one of them. I have a miserable room hard by: if you wish to walk a few steps I can offer you a better glass of whiskey than you will get in any club, and then I shall endeavour to assuage your unusual, and I confess," he added with a flash of vanity, "pardonable curiosity."

"Willingly," cried Mr Vellery, who no more thought of shirking a mysterious encounter than he did "timber" when he went a-hunting. Accordingly, at the word, he walked away in the other's guidance. As for the stranger, though he was indeed confident enough before, he had taken a manifest increase of assurance within the last minute; for there is scarcely a knowledge more bracing than when a man learns that the world, even though it be represented, as in this case, by a mere hazardous passer, finds his face and demeanour so remarkable that it indulges in quick speculation upon the events of his life. The two had not proceeded more than a few hundred yards, when they turned into a quiet street and paused before a neat clean house. The stranger opened the door with a key, and having lit a candle at the stair-foot, he led Mr Vellery to the second landing. Here Mr Vellery was requested to enter a decent room which although it was not large, yet altogether belied the adjective which the occupier had stuck to it in the street. It was furnished with respectable comfort; and as no bed was to be seen, but a door which opened into another room showed a bed in there, Mr Vellery concluded that his acquaintance, notwithstanding his poor mouth, enjoyed the luxury of two rooms, and while he slept in that, varied the idle hours he had mentioned in this one. There were a few books lying about, which Mr Vellery, as he glanced at the titles, found to be mostly socialistic and anarchistic works in French and German.

The host, meanwhile, busied himself very hospitably to draw some glasses from a cupboard, and these he now placed before Mr Vellery, and also a bottle without a label. This contained whiskey which, when he had tasted it, Mr Vellery decided to be some of the softest and most mature he had ever drunk in his life.

"I saw you looking at my books," remarked the other, with an indulgent and somewhat condescending smile. "I confess that when I do read, and it is not often, I read to study: I do not waste my time and my health upon the fatuities of the renowned Mrs Ardour, or your other fashionable novelists.—And now," he pursued, stretching out his legs and lighting a pipe of tobacco, "I will narrate without prologue the main facts of my deplorable existence—that is, if you feel yourself at ease, and can endure for a short time the change from the marble halls and the gilded saloons wherein you evidently reside, to the squalid chamber of the unfortunate."

Mr Vellery was one of the people who (happily or unhappily, as the reader chooses to look at the matter) are wholly unable to retort briskly upon an impertinent remark, or one, such as the above, in distressing taste. So he was fain to smile, and wave his hand in a vague gesture of assent.

Chapter IV

"My name," began the stranger, "is Argan."

"What!" cried Mr Vellery with a start. "Are you Argan the Nihilist?"

The other pointed to his breast with a smile of intense gratification, and bowed.

"My name," he replied, "is Argan—Labour Argan. Will you tell me yours?"

"Undoubtedly," said the guest. "My name is Shawlcoat Vellery."

"I've never heard of you," quoth the other bluntly. "My ridiculous fore-name I owe to a whim of my father, who, not content with forcing me into this loathsome world, must plaister me with a name which has been my curse and stultifies all my theories. For before we go any further, I'll have you know that I am not a friend of work. There is something radically wrong in the organization of the earth, since men have to work for a living. The churches tell us that by sin work was brought into the world; but to accept that position is to ascribe to the Governor of the Universe the malevolence of a devil, or the insouciance of a fool: for are not the diseases, bereavements, despairs, and death which mankind undergo a sufficient punishment for sin,—even granting that sin, which was certainly foreknown and by consequence fore-ordained, deserved any punishment at all? Can anything be more foolish than to impute to God the kind of domination and method of punishment and reward which men exercise over other men? But if I thought that God did, in reality and with deliberation, send the greatest part of men into the world to observe them minutely while they sweated and rotted, and afterwards to plunge them into hell, then," shouted Argan, bouncing on the table with his fist, "I should consider Him a lousy tyrant! And as it is the duty of every man who lives under a bad government by all means to hamper and make impossible that government, so would it be the duty of men to deny and break the laws of so cruel a God. If God is what your churches declare, it delights me to think of the state of festering rebellion against Him which the world is in at present. He deserves no better. For since a love of freedom is planted in the breast of every man, can a more fiendish cruelty and monstrous abomination be raked out of the pit of hell, than that He who has created this love of freedom should Himself flourish the heaviest whip, Himself impose an eternal yoke, Himself be the most implacable and relentless of tyrants. In truth, this conception of God, fostered by the Old Testament, and then by St Paul, Calvin, Ignatius the Jesuit, and the like, is so terrible and intolerable that men when they come to the pinch, when there exists not a thing between their bare souls and God, instinctively abandon it: and the wretches in hospital, in prison, in the trenches, turn from the inhumanity of men to the humanity of God; for they feel that He comprehends, as no fellow-man possibly can, the crushing effect of the accumulated miseries of life. And this being so, how small must the greatest of man's sins appear before God's pitying and tolerant eyes! Now, since I feel thus, I cannot allow any teacher of scholastic theology to compel me to believe that my chief purpose in the world is to do brutalizing and annoying work for several hours every day, to benefit others or to keep their minds easy; even as a mother's mind is easy when she knows her child is busily engaged with a toy, for she thinks at that moment he is not likely to set fire to the house. I do not say that a man should not work to get control of the herd, or for some other great end, though I myself do not perceive an end which is worth an hour's toil; but I do say, that if a man be working out of sight of a competent reward, and since the greatest part must unfortunately work to get bread, he should get as much out of his employer, and do as little for him as he can. And I positively assert, there is no moral obligation upon a man to work; and all the reproaches flung at idlers are but perverse inventions which affect only weak and gregarious beings—the dupes of those who know they would be undone if my notions generally prevailed. You yourself, I take it, are an upholder of the principle of work; and I am the more sure of this because you look like one of the class that never does a stroke itself, but employs others to work for its comfort."

"Yes; I think I am," replied Mr Vellery, finding himself directly questioned. "I haven't thought much about the matter, but I think work is a good healthy thing. It prevents people from getting a lot of rubbish and morbid trash into their heads. I know I have found that myself. You see, most people are happier when they are working than when they are idling. You are not half so bored when you are at work, as you are when you are sitting down twiddling your thumbs. Besides, it keeps a man out of mischief."

"'Tis false, Vellery," cried Argan flatly, with every sign of strong excitement. "'Tis a damned lie! So far is what you say from being true, that it is impossible to gauge the infinite varieties of mischief which are created by work. Who gets into more mischief, who fills the police-courts, the working classes, or the idle classes? Most men hate and envy their employers, and their vanity is offended by every wage they get because they think they are worth more. Look at the numbers of apprentices in all ages who have murdered their masters. Look at the strikes, look at the riots in foundries and mines. Consider the mortal rivalry between two men engaged in the same trade. These are only a few of the calamities which are brought about by work."

"I see you want to remodel from its foundations a system of life which for centuries has been found endurable," said Mr Vellery. "You are a Socialist."

Argan's eyes darkened. "You have offered me without provocation the worst affront in your vocabulary," he declared. "Don't say that again, Vellery, my man. It might be dangerous. There's a revolver in that drawer."

"Oh, well," says Mr Vellery, smiling and entertained by the other's humour, "it seems to me that Anarchism and Socialism come to about the same thing in the end. They both want to do away with all that makes life pleasant and civilized."

"Now there you're wrong, Vellery," replied Argan. "You're dead wrong, my little Tory. I pass over the last part of your somewhat hasty speech because we are not likely to agree upon what makes life civi-lized—or pleasant either, for the matter of that. But permit me to show you the difference between Socialists and Anarchists, by an instance culled," quoth Argan gravely, "from a wide field of experience.—One fine morning I was on my walks in Paris through one of those streets which horsemen take to gain the *Bois*. Now, there chanced to pass a young gentleman with a self-conscious air, somewhat over-dressed, mounted upon a showy horse which he caused most needlessly to curvet and prance, doubtless with the silly notion that he was stirring the admiration and awe of the foot-passers, whereas in truth he was but moving them to envy and hatred. For look ye, Vellery, there is no city which marks so plain what wealth can do as Paris, and therefore, since the poor people have continually before their eyes the advantages of wealth which they themselves can by no means attain, so do they loathe the possessors; and I would hazard it is owing to this propensity of the Paris rich, which has always existed, to spend their money out of doors, so to speak, in the sight of the people, that Paris can plume herself upon the greatest rebellion ever witnessed of the poor against the rich. But leaving the general, let me recall that as my young gentleman passed, a podgy old man with a wallet slung over his shoulder, who was evidently taking a morning message from one house of business to another, stopped on the causeway and began to yell and scream insults and curses at the equestrian. 'Look at him, the idler!' shrieks out my old man, mad with fury. 'The dirty good-for-nothing! Ah, what a horrible sight! Horror! horror!' he raves with his hand to his mouth. Hereupon, conquering my natural repugnance to speak to people I don't know, I stepped up to the shouter. 'Why,' I asked, 'are you so incensed against yonder gentleman?' 'Ah, the wretch!' replied the old fellow passionately, 'the miserable wretch! He goes gaily about enjoying himself with the money which ought to belong to the poor. They all get their pleasure with the money which ought to belong to the poor—all of them who go rolling down the Avenue in their fine carriages showing off their dresses,—yes indeed, the dresses of the loathsome sweaty women who plaister themselves with cosmetics and perfumes because they are too lazy and unclean to keep their skins healthy with cold water.' From this speech I concluded, as no doubt you will, that my friend followed with reluctance an employment in some commercial house which made its chief profit out of articles for the toilet of more or less elegant madams. However, I did not notice aloud what I had perceived, but contented myself with this replique: 'Let us, sir, by your leave, attach ourselves to the main question. Now that I come to regard him attentively, there can be little doubt that your young gentleman on the horse is only a gentleman of the night-before-last, if not of yesterday. But let that be granted, and yet how can you pretend that he squanders the money which belongs to the poor? Let us suppose that his relatives got their fortunes by gas—yes, when I gaze upon his somewhat luminous costume I am convinced that he is the Gas:—the Gas which rings with such persistent and outrageous regularity at the door of every citizen, disturbing the weary father when he is embracing his children and thinking of a café where some one attends him at the second turning to the left; agonizing the wife when she is arranging her hair in a new fashion and examining the folds of a new bed-gown which shall be seen by no other eyes but her husband's;—the Gas, I say, which ever presents its bill at a wrong moment, causing ignoble rows, ruining the peace of families. Well, I repeat this young gentleman's relatives have got a fortune by the positive regularity of their appearances with gas-bills; and yet how does it follow that their money belongs to the poor? For look you, they have not compelled the poor to burn gas; on the contrary, there is nothing in the wide world to prevent all the poor in Paris to-night from burning candles, from burning oil, from burning nothing at all.'"

"Or newspapers," quoth Mr Vellery.

"Or newspapers—just so, Vellery," assented Argan. "I thought they were covered by the third alternative I gave. Well, the old fellow stood somewhat at a loss after my speech; he was frankly gravelled and undone: then he blundered out with, 'But that young brute does no work. There is work enough to go round. There is work for all men, and all men must do that work!' he cries out with a good imitation of the Socialist orators—nay, so strong was the mimic in him that he actually drew his handkerchief to sponge his forehead largely, as he had seen his orators do on platforms. 'Work!' I exclaimed at him, for I was piqued (says Argan) by his senile depravity. 'Work!—Know sir, that the man who gets all he can without working in your narrow sense, or— when for the moment there is nothing to get—chooses a most pleasant spot in a public park and lives happily and idly through the long day watching the shadows grow, the birds playing with the leaves, hearing the plash of water in some distant grove, and letting the wind come sweetly about his face, this man has every whit as much right (since he has been put into the world against his will) to the sun, and the wind, and the pleasures of the earth that you have—you, or any other worker. Truly (says I) it has ever been a great pleasure for me to pass in the forenoon through a public park of any great city; because at that time in those places may be found the wholesome worthy patterns of patient idlers. At an hour when in a great town the most of men are moiling and sweating, these sit on the benches with their hands in their pockets. Some doze; some examine languidly the sky and moving clouds; some read the papers of many evenings ago; they care for nothing. Now you, on the other hand, have worked—worked in a close shop till your liver has become diseased and the bile has mounted to your head and yellowed your eyes. Therefore you rage at people for possessing the wealth you have not been clever enough to acquire, and all you are fit for and able to do'—quoth I damning him heartily—'is to stand in the public street and bawl against a harmless if conceited youth in gas-coloured clothes. If you yourself became rich to-morrow, as others like you have become, you would bellow as loud (though not in the open street, which would be something gained) against the rapacity, and extortions, and general nuisance of the poor. I can see you with a shiny hat and heavy watch-chain in the lobby of the Parliament House swelling out and puffing:—People of my position must protect themselves against the encroachments of the rabble. Ah, Baron, these poor, what ingrates! I know them, know them down to their toe-nails.—I see your eyes glisten (I said to him) at the picture: my compliments; may you arrive!—Now on the other side, my idlers don't waste their time in bilious gabble and unprofitable envy:—no, they dare to act, and what is more they dare to die. Sycophant newspapers grovelling to the bourgeois and people with incomes call them sullen, cowards—what else? But it does not need a very keen intellect to remark that *coward* is hardly the word for a man who, inspired by his cause, for the sake of an idea, commits an act wholly intellectual wherein not the least spark of passion or sensual pleasure enters, an act for which he knows he must certainly perish—and perish, mind you, without that assurance, so precious to the weakness of men in dire straits, that a great body of mankind sympathize with him, or at least pity him. The truth is,' I added, laying a forefinger on the old fellow's waistcoat, 'you are merely a Socialist. I'—I said—'I am an Anarchist.' Even as I spoke these words, Vellery, two policemen came lounging across the street; and no sooner had my old Socialist spied them than he saluted briefly, and lancing a look of terror at me as he drew off, took himself hastily away. I remember him still for two things;—for besides that he illustrated the futility and inconsequence of the usual Socialist, I took from his company a hardened conviction of the crabbed and ruinous effect of regular work.

"But this subject," continued Argan, musing a little, "interesting as it is, still is not the one I promised to discourse upon; and I have been inveigled into it by the fury which possesses me whenever I think of my unwholesome and ludicrous name. My name, as I have told you, is—"

However, as I have filled up a chapter with as much as it can conveniently hold, I would think it an awkward miscarriage so ill to order affairs as not to put an end to it here and now. I am informed, indeed, that the learned W-n-s-t, in his elaborate treatise upon the Literary Art, strongly condemns the division of chapters in a short narrative or essay, which he declares, seriously disturbs the harmony that should exist in the reader's mind: and I understand he further maintains (for I've not had time to look into him myself) that no elegant writer, and no one, in sooth, but some profligate and abandoned scribe who has no good name to lose, would ever introduce chapters, save in a book of about two folio volumes—which, Heaven help us! is the exact size of the critic's own.

No.

Now, I do not intend to dispute this matter; for there is no wise man but would bear a great deal rather than make a bustle. Besides, among ourselves, you and I know that your great reputations are not always to be gotten by intelligence alone, and not a few professors resemble the fantastic gentleman of Turin, whom nothing would serve but he must set up for a Master of Dance, though he was so lame that he could hardly go or stand.

Chapter V

"My name," quoth the stranger, "is Argan."

"I shall remember," says Mr Vellery, with a smile and a nod of the head.

Now 'tis the most grievous thing in life that Mr Vellery could not have kept quiet at that moment; for by throwing out this remark he tripped up the other, who was coming on fairly, and brought him to a dead stop. The truth is, that just as a runner sometimes digs for his backward foot a hole in the cinder-path wherefrom he can bound into his stride, so the host needed the spring communicated by this *exordium* or proemial phrase to set him a-going. He pish-ed, pshaw-ed, ran his hand over his bead, blew his nose, got up and moved about the room, and then came back and threw himself with a swag into his chair.—And at this corner I would take you aside for a whisper, that we are often prone (which is a manner of saying,—You may not be, but

I am) to let some trifle or buzz by a stretch of condescension into our heads, where it soon becomes easy of the building, cheats and plays the wag with our judgment, till ere long it comes to be master; and then— heigh-ho, jerry! there's no travelling without his Worship. I knew one man who was as mum as a cod-fish till he was sitting; I knew another who could never speak till he was—nay, as you like it!—spitting. Some are but stutterers till they get to their feet; and other some (praise be!) are no good till they are cheek by jowl in bed.

"My name," he declared, "is Argan."

A thousand plagues seize it! I contend this would vex any flesh alive. Are we never to get on, morning, noon, or night! Here we have been backing and filling for more than half-an-hour; and just when, after a host of difficulties, I get matters arranged for a fair start, I find that my pen, so please ye, will mark no more than a log of wood, and I must chase after a goose till she drops a plume, and cut a new one. I vow I will write no more till I am in a better temper, and that won't be to-day; so I'll go out into the world and enjoy myself.

⌢

I had, last night after I went out, a most diverting jocund adventure. As I was going through the wood which lies on the side of the hill less than a mile from here, I saw, in the 'tween lights, a flutter of white—

But I find that this pen marks neatly enough, so I had better be stirring in the main business.

Chapter VI

"My name," he said, "is Argan: Labour Argan. My father, who was a dissenting minister at Caistor in Lincolnshire, loaded me with this name because my mother was brought to bed of me with great pain and danger; and my father, a person of dismal and unbalanced character, was wont to assert that throughout the crisis he wrestled mightily in prayer, and his wrestlings prevailed. But that you may perceive his solicitude for my mother's life did not restrain his desires, I need only mention that I am the fourth child of eleven. With the eleventh child, in fact, my mother abandoned her wrestler and this world. Perhaps her life was happy, and perhaps unhappy: I cannot tell: it depends upon whether her senses required more gratification than her mind. She had not been dead many years when I was sent to a school kept by the Methodists at Brigg. Here I learned nothing but a disgust for cant and whine which has served me through life. When I was about fifteen, notwithstanding the restraint and oppression to which I was subjected, my natural force of character began to assert itself. I remember that one day I smashed the window of a baker in the town, who refused to let me have some cakes which I promised to pay him for within a month. My schoolmaster had the good sense to see in this the natural explosion of a high spirit; and I believe he paid for the window himself. My next exploit, however, he had too narrow a mind to regard with a lenient eye. The old fellow had in his house a very comely serving-wench upon whom, as I was precocious, and my passions sprang early, I had cast many a languishing glance. I discovered her room; and one night, about twelve o'clock, I introduced myself into her bed. But the girl, either because she was virtuous, or (what is more probable) because I was not the one she wanted, before I touched her set up a howl to crack the ceiling, and brought the entire household about my ears. I can still laugh when I recall the apparition of the schoolmaster—doddered with age, in a short night-shirt which showed his withered shanks, holding his trousers in one hand, his long beard blowing over his shoulder, coughing and puffing, his face furious and bemused. He was flanked by his fat trubtail of a wife in a long white gown, with spectacles to her nose, who held a candle; and supported by his two scarecrow daughters, and the rest of the servants; while some of the boys, who thought me a prodigious fine fellow, stood sniggering in the rear. Before such a squadron, there was nothing for me but unconditional surrender. Ha, ha, ha," cried Argan in a revel of mirth, "I swear to God it's monstrous funny. Can't you laugh, Vellery?"

"If you appeal to me," said Mr Vellery, "I'm bound to say I see little to laugh at in what you have just told me."

"That's because you have no sense of humour, Vellery," responded the other with a truculent smile. "You've got too much buckram about you; you are too stiff and precise."

Mr Vellery's heart smote him as he listened to this, for he recognized the same note of complaint he had always heard when he was in the company of desperate sinners.

"You should supple yourself a bit," pursued Argan in a domineering tone. "You live too much in your own class. Men like you when they call themselves tired of life are generally only tired of theatres. You ought to shake a leg, and see the rough world as I have done."

"I hope," said Mr Vellery, drolling him, "that you are not one of those tedious persons who have a passion for making every one else like themselves, and are impatient of differences."

"No—not at all," replied Argan, a little taken aback. "Not at all. When I advise you to see the world, I don't mean you should see it in the way I have seen it, nor do I think that at the end of it you would be the kind of man I am. I don't think so, Vellery," quoth Argan, pursing up his lips with a touch of pomposity; "I do not think so. I began young. Indeed, I may say my wanderings in the world began that very night of the row at school; for old *Grief and Pain,* after a lengthy discourse of Moralities, did not waste much ceremony to let me know that he hoped to have his house free of me by the morning. As I knew the dirty weather it would make if I cast up at my father's in such a story, and as I had long desired the life of a sailor, I resolved to mould circumstances with my own hands; and instead of seeking bread and water and a volume of sermons, I set out for the docks at Grimsby.

"I believe," continued Argan, passing his hand across his face, "I believe I could make an interesting story of those early experiences of mine at Grimsby. But it would be too long for this time; so I will merely tell you that at length I got a berth as steward's mate in a small brig trading to Valparaiso and the Falklands. I tumbled from ship to ship for better than four years, till I found myself in the forecastle of a clipper in the China trade.

"I remark this ship because it was aboard of her I encountered the man who formed my character, if"—said Argan, giving just such a flourish with his right arm as would send any mumpish self-distrust that might be lurking near, round the corner at a quick march; "if it can be truly asserted that any man has formed a character as strong and original as my own, But if I acknowledge any master, it is he and no other; and at least he gave a direction to my thoughts and set them going. He was second mate in the ship, and he was known to have, as we used to say, a bit of reading. Doubtless he found me intelligent, for he picked me out, and in his spare time gave me some instruction. His father was a Frenchman, and his mother a German, and he had served his time in English ships, so he had a good command of three languages. We called him Mr Faber: his real name, I suppose, was Fabre. I never knew any man who had for his fellow-men a greater loathing and contempt. He told me that he tried more and more to resemble horses in their sense, their cleanliness, courage, and honesty; and that whenever he felt he was acting as well as he could like a horse, and by consequence unlike a man, he felt proud. For all that, he was civil enough to those under him, and popular with the crew. He was as brave as fire. I have known him go aloft in a squall, when many of your heroes would be crying for their mammies.

"I saw him save the lives of two men in my time. One was a pretty bad case and took some pluck. We were lying fairly well becalmed in a water alive with sharks. One of the hands, Toby Ames, a man who couldn't swim, was painting the starboard quarter-boat, when he missed his footing on the poop-rail, and went overboard. The men stood all with their mouths gaping open, looking pretty green and lubberly, and the captain who was on deck roared out to clear away a boat, when Mr Faber put his head through the forehatch and gripped the matter at a glance. He had heavy eyebrows, and sharpish eyes, and a rather bitter mouth, and he looked about him at all of us in a kind of jeer. "By Christ!" he says, just like that;—"by Christ!" and with that he off with his coat, and over he went, and held Toby up till they lowered the boat. I have often thought since, when I have read of knights of the olden time who went into battle calling mildly on the name of Christ, that while of course they used it as a delicate prayer, and he only as a rough sailorman's oath, perhaps not one of those gentlemen had a purer or braver heart than poor common old Faber. He told me afterwards that he was sorry he had saved the man, because he had no spite against him personally. That was the way he used to talk. He died of a surfeit, brought on by drinking seventeen glasses of Holland gin on end for a wager, while we lay careening at Frederick-Henry Island, off New Guinea; and I remember as if it was yesterday, that when we had tied his body to a plank and were burying him in the sand on the beach, how the crabs kept hopping into the grave. A few of these books belonged to him; that's one of them near you—not that one—the one by your elbow. His memory is in benediction," said Argan, taking a pull at the whiskey. "Here's to his ghost! Poor devil! there's not much else left of him now.

"After his death I continued six or seven years at sea, and each year my disgust of the human race increased. There was not then, as there is not now a man or a woman on earth whom I value a biscuit. It is not that I am a misanthrope or bearish; but I confess I am unable to work up sympathy with those who are indifferent to me."

"'Tis much the same thing," said Mr Vellery smiling.

"Yes, perhaps it is," replied Argan after a pause. "However that may be, my sense of the horror and futility of life grew to such a point, that at length I determined to run the ship I chanced then to be in, and every soul aboard, to the bottom."

"What a man!" cried Mr Vellery, lost in admiration. "Here's a fellow!"

"I had not long to wait for an opportunity. We were coming on the Alio Islands in the filthiest, worst-handled ship that ever carried a main-brace. The captain was a heavy, brutal ruffian, who spent his time playing poker for the shirt on his back with the first mate in the aft cabin. Regularly, about three bells in the middle of the night they would start up from the table and fall to giving each other every rogue and rascal they could lay their tongues to. Then they would step out on deck and dodge about a bit, each trying to be first to hit the other a whack on the jaw. If the ship was rolling, they would tumble, close-gripped, biting and kicking, into the scuppers. After they had strangled and tore for a few minutes, they would get up and shake themselves and turn in; and the next day they would be at the cards the same as ever. One night the captain laid the mate's face open with a tumbler; another night the mate broke the captain's finger as they tussled; but it made no difference to the next day's gamble. They never spoke a civil word to one another that I ever heard of; and yet day by day for mortal weary months they seriously faced each other over a dirty pack of cards. The ship was sailed by the second mate, who was a half-black from New Orleans.

"Every seaman who knows those latitudes is aware that the Alio group has as ugly a coast to come on as there is in the world. There is a big sunken reef to the nor'-nor'-west, and there are others which are not marked in ordinary charts. Many a captain would not dare to take off his boots for a day and a night when he was bearing down on Alio; but our old man was of a different complexion, and refused to interrupt his game in the cabin. As I was known to have been in two or three times before, I was put to do a trick at the wheel; and Stovey—that was the second mate—who knew rather less about bringing the ship in than he did about driving a coach-and-four from London to York, took the quarter-deck. Now, as I was the only man aboard, except the captain himself, who had the bearings of the coast, my plan was to wear the ship round gradually and bring her down upon the reefs, and then we might chant *De Profundis*! And everything, mark you, was in my favour. There was a fine strong gale blowing dead on the land, and a high white sea running. As the ship took in a good deal of water to leeward, we had stowed the yards and double-reefed the main-sail, and yet were making good way. Everything, I repeat, was in my favour; when by an extraordinary chance in those waters, about half-past two in the afternoon a tramp steamer hove in sight on the port bow, and before I had watched her long I discovered that she was steering the exact course I had marked for myself. The second mate, when he made the steamer, ran down to the cabin and brought the 'old man' up on deck. This one, after he had sized up the steamer through his glass for a good space, walked aft to look at the compass. No sooner did he see how his own ship was standing, than he God-damned me for a lousy swab, hit me a kick, and seizing the nearest thing to his hand, which happened to be a chain, he struck me with so much force on the head, that I fell stunned to the deck.

"'Stand by there, ye greasy lubbers, and fly a signal to that tramp!' sang out the captain. 'She may sight it or she may not, but she's goin' to her death as sure as onions. And so might we be, all owing to that groggy son of a sojer over there, if I hadn't been on deck doing my duty. You've got a good captain, my sonnies, and don't you forget to remember it. As for you, Pete Stovey, Esquire, M.P., you black-hearted buck black, you're on the voyage for your health, I suppose? What do you mean by walking about with your hands in your pockets like a half-pay officer and never looking at the course? By God, if I don't learn you what it is to take a quarter-deck before the middle watch—my name ain't Captain, that's all.'

"Whether the steamer did not note our signal or neglected it, she held on her course, and so there was nothing left for us but to attend the catastrophe. We had not long to wait. The steamer, which was making not less than ten knots through the water, drove directly on the reefs, and (as I judge from the great volley of steam that burst from her hold) immediately split. All on board perished, save three of the crew who had made a shift to get clear of the steamer in a boat; and these we picked up after cruising about for more than two hours. From these men we learned that their captain, although an old navigator of the island waters, had steered the precise course which I myself intended, and had in fact, either from a sudden accession of madness, or some obscure wish to consummate a crime, foundered his own ship. Mine was the idea: he was the triumphant executor. If I had but known it, that affair of the steamer was the first symptom of the malign spell which has weighed upon me through life, and whereof there is more to be related.

"When the ship was paid at Sydney, I was put ashore, but not before the captain had given me a keel-hauling and broke many hard words over my back. I was now grown weary of the sea, so I decided to make for England and try what I could do on land. When I arrived at London, I found by chance that I had been advertised for in the newspapers at intervals for above a year. It turned out that an aunt of mine who hated my father had chosen to leave me, having always heard me defamed by him, two small farms in Yorkshire;—and this she did not from love of the son, but from contempt of the father. Since that time the income from those farms has enabled me to live in irksome, but, I trust, decent poverty—such as you witness here," quoth Argan with a spacious wave of the hand.

"I now began to have a sense of the advantage to be gained from a long visit to the great cities of the Continent, and therefore, after some uncertain removes from place to place, I cast anchor for a good while at Rome. But time, and a close acquaintance with nations, only served to make plainer to me the strength of the sordid herd-instinct in mankind. Almost every man in every nation wishes to go with the crowd; scarcely a man has the force to stand out and say: 'I will be *one*.' Of course the man who goes with the crowd is what we call a 'law-abiding citizen'; but 'law-abiding', unfortunately means in many cases, drugged and stupefied by the law. Of that, though you seem to demur, there can be little question, Vellery; and I will produce two instances to prove and explain what I am now advancing.

"And first, with relation to 'law-abiding citizens' who, I say, are stupefied by the law. I never realized so palpably what the mass will stand from an old bellwether who holds his position without any qualification for it that God or man can respect, as I did when about ten years ago I read a notice posted in no less awful a place than a cathedral. This notice even in a profane theatre would have been indecent; in a church it was abominable, overbearing and scandalous. Indeed, at a theatre, a notice so conceived would have had little toleration; but as we have not yet come to regard the managers of theatres with the same respect as bishops and deans, what would have been refused in the play-house was accepted in the church. And, I think, the reason is easy to be assigned; for while the thousands of people who read that notice must have thought uncomfortably, perhaps sub-consciously, it was wrong, they nevertheless at the same time thought clearly and consciously:—It is the will of our Superiors; and drugged by that thought passed on, letting my lords the honest Superiors carry the point as they pleased. The notice in question stated in the most arrogant and brutal terms that all packages of people who entered the cathedral, and even a coat carried loose on the arm, would be seized and examined by the police. Police! there's a word to seize the eye and dwell with you in a building whereof I suppose they have not just yet altogether given up the pretence that it is kept open for the public worship of One who led a great holy life among poor sailormen, among the despised of towns, and the horror of the genteel, castaways, disinherited, wrecks—yes, the word *Police, Police, Police*, in every corner; never the word *God* that I could see in the whole place. And indeed in every direction walked policemen: and they are walking still, for what I know, to keep us in orderly minds, lest in our devotional moments we be so carried away by the Kingdom of Heaven that we forget the Church Militant, and rich tactless deans abhorrent of the low kind of people who have no advantage in the state by themselves or their relations to make them a yielding ground for flattery—forget them alas! and more heinous still, forget dragooning prelates who deign to address the common herd only in insolent words of threat and command. To be sure, yon cathedral does not move a man to say his prayers there any more than the Stock Exchange does: you feel instinctively that the Spirit of God has long since gone out of that unholy museum, and left the Devil to amaze himself by watching an exhibition of Deans backed up by the Police in a desecrated church. But suppose, Vellery—I admit 'tis a wild and fantastical notion, but suppose a ragged man or woman, doubtless of low character, whom the coachman of the Prelate, or the Dean, or any of the Chapter would ruthlessly drive down, and who would be thrown out if they were found loitering about the Close—suppose such a ragged man or woman to enter that church, and then—and then—suddenly they are stirred to turn from this world where all is so bitter, where nobody cares, where the kind quiet words are so few, where they are constantly being kicked and cursed away from people's doors—this broken tramp, this degraded whore, are moved to say a word from the depths of their sealed hearts to One who will listen, who will not laugh or grow angry, who will sympathize and understand. And so they kneel down and begin their mean shambling prayers, and for the relief of it drop their miserable bundles, which they have carried all day, on the floor. Consider then, Vellery, the sudden apparition of the policeman—hauling these dangerous malefactors from their knees, bursting open the miserable parcels, and to the wretched plea of the unclean woman whom every right-minded person should of course spit at, bringing it out as she does in a hoarse voice, with a sob, and a lonely coughing enough to render up her soul—her plea, 'I was only a-sayin' my prayers, sir,'—remark the sublime answer supported by the war-strength of Prelate, Dean, and Chapter; 'I tell you this ain't a place to pray in—leastwise for the likes o' you.' Ah Vellery, cannot you see what pleasure such an action would give to God, performed upon filthy suspected scum by His jealous agents? Think of the new glory for our holy religion; the triumph of our gracious faith; the new proof of the personal appeal which Christianity makes to the most obdurate; the new sense of peace and relief in their religion experienced by the outcast woe-fallen man and woman who have been collared by the police; the rejoicing of the angels—yea, even the angels in helmets and top-hats.—Jesus Christ would have struck down those notices," Argan went on, putting a match to his pipe. "I tell you he would, Vellery. They were matters of that kind in the Temple of Jerusalem which made him burn with rage and scorn. I think his opinion would be, that it were better all the architecture in the world should perish, than one poor soul be harassed and brow-beaten for the sake of it. Christ, I say, would have destroyed those placards in that cathedral, and he would have been laid by the heels in the county gaol, and all the prelates, and deans, and chapters, and magistrates, and county magnates—yes, and journalists, don't let us forget them, would have bullied the life out of him for a scurvy revolutionist. And all the world would be content, nor would a whisper be heard on the other side; because the prosecutors would represent the law, and the populace, too willing to take things for granted, too stupefied, and dazed, and frightened by the law to dream the law may be in error, would repeat: Who are we to urge, when our betters have spoken;—a dupery so lively and infectious that I regret to confess there are times when it reaches up from the street and poisons even me in this garret.

"And if you would examine my second statement," Argan resumed, after he had hit the coal-box an enthusiastic kick, as though it were a cathedral full of his enemies,—"the herd-instinct of mankind, I'll ask you to consider the eagerness of men for a leader; that is, for someone to take the responsibility: they will jump at the first man who offers. That is why so many countries are in the hands of the second-rate. Neither is it so difficult to retain the office of leader as is generally supposed:—no; rather what sets the thinking man to wonder is that the crowd ever summons the resolution to overthrow even a notoriously bad leader, since it feels the need of him so much, and by so doing is acting against its nature; just as it is hard to imagine your 'law-abiding citizen' with nerve enough to knock down a policeman in uniform, even though he detect him in an outrageous violation of the law. Nor is it difficult to understand the ascendance a bad leader, even a knave and impostor, with sufficient effrontery and self-reliance, gains over the crowd: for the crowd in proportion to its credulity loves affirmations, and does not dislike brutal solutions. It mistrusts those men who hesitate, question, balance, who fear to step out freely lest they step into the mud. It wishes to see a precise end: and the man who has never learned from history to distrust his particular notions and allow there are two sides to every question, and three to most; who has never by human learning shaped his understanding to acknowledge his private weaknesses and the dull ignorance of the people;—such a man sees but one end, and admitting no doubt or contradiction, there he leads the crowd. That is why great scholars or thinkers, I might even say fully educated men, have seldom been seen as leaders of the populace: they weigh, they reason, fall out of sympathy with violent assertions, become disgusted or half-hearted, and the crowd sees through them.—No; a man to lead the crowd must be authoritative, obstinate, rigid in self-belief, a bar of iron. The crowd thus led by the ears is utterly despicable and chicken-hearted; but it is also not without pathos. For what, after all—oh, what in the world is more pathetic than a great crowd, with its stupidity, its blindness, its huddled fear as at the Last Judgment, its dull loyalty, its utter dependence on its units, its mute appeal for a guide! 'Tis when you see a crowd watching an army pass, that you perceive what discipline, organized by a few superior minds, and carried out by average trained minds, can do. Without discipline the army would be as weak and childish as the crowd.

"In England, I am bound to confess—and you must know me well enough by this time to be sure I am not troubled by any nonsensical scruples of patriotism, or designedly civil because I am talking to an Englishman—but I assert that in England this bondage to the law and helpless reliance on the mob-leader are less prominent than in some other nations, though it is the common gibe on the Continent to point to us as the chief example of these very things. There is, doubtless, in England amongst a certain class, a class which may be said to begin with the banker, and end with the retail grocer, and includes doctors, solicitors, authors, farmers, and the like, a horrible and shameless abjection before mere rank and title, entirely removed from an orderly respect. However, if you substitute money for rank, which after all is pretty much the same thing, since they both stand for power, and 'tis the power they represent the poor creatures dimly perceive and worship;—well, if you substitute money for rank you will find this same miserable abasement in almost all the nations of Christendom. Now, the poison of this ignoble adulation is, that it encourages the loud and brutal insolence of the worshipped: as all the world wants to copy them, their coarse notions prevail, and by consequence we have an age with the shabbiest, most material ideals and crudest aspirations known to history. If you think that remains to be proved, Vellery, I would invite you to consider modern architecture. The later nineteenth century architecture is a perfect epitome of the defects and vulgar sins of this age. It is flaunting, self-assertive, and protests in every line that it cost an incredible sum of money, and wants you to be aware of that. Take as an example the walk from the Invalides in Paris across the new bridge and on to the Champs-Élysées. When you get to the Champs-Élysées you are well prepared by your walk for the over-dressed, self-conscious women in carriages. Or take the new parts of any of the ancient, dignified Italian or German cities, where the houses seem to have been run up to keep the steam-tram from feeling lonely. Or consider above all that sad Berlin, with its aggressive park, and terrible streets where each building looks like either an hotel with six lifts, or a bank, from which (you know not why) you expect every moment to hear burst forth the clang of a brass band.—I maintain the cause of all this abomination is the worship of wealth and rank by what are called the middle classes, and the consequent humble acceptance by the general of the mediocre taste and arrogance of their poor gods. Many years ago, in a book of Faber's, I came across some remarks of a man of the seventeenth century, the Marquess of Halifax, on this very matter. I don't know who he was, or what he did, but his observations pleased me so much that I got them by heart. Here they are," said Argan; and he continued, dragging over his words like the old fellow in a country tavern who drones out the newspaper to his neighbours:—"'Some make quality an idol, and then their reason must fall down and worship it; they would have the world think that no amends can ever be made for the want of a great title or an ancient coat of arms; they imagine that with these advantages they stand upon the higher ground, which maketh them look down upon merit and virtue as things inferior to them. This mistake is not only senseless, but criminal too, in putting a greater price upon that which is a piece of good luck, than upon things which are valuable in themselves. Laughing is not enough for such a folly; it must be severely whipped, as it justly deserves.'—Read ostentatious, parading millionaires and their families into that," declared Argan, banging at the grate with a poker, "and it fits very well to-day."

Mr Vellery looked a little overpowered. "I have always thought," he said, "that the people who are constantly girding at high rank are just those who are uneasy and uncertain about their own position. If a man is sure of himself, and values himself, he doesn't bother his head about other people."

"I don't suppose that can apply to my Marquess, however," replied Argan with a touch of defiance. "I take it that you are one of the class which (if it were put to it) would regard the vehement denunciations of rank and wealth in the Gospels as shrill and overdone, a blot of snobbery upon an otherwise unblemished performance. And this reminds me to mention that English class in which you will find a foolish and evil worship of what, in its jargon, is called 'good form,' whereof the result is to blur and ruin individual character: and the contemplation of this miserable and pestilent affectation leads me to the paradox that the final vulgarity is to be a gentleman.—But," said Argan, sheering off from that argument, to Mr Vellery's great relief, "these things are only surface maladies, confined to special classes, and not serious; while, on the other hand, there is hardly a trace in England of that degraded and servile cringing before ignorant, overbearing, and brutal louts who have been hoisted by political machinations into petty offices for which they are unfit, that obsequious and imploring demeanour before mere froth and mud which you can perceive in those vaunted Republics, France and the United States. And as for France, you will note that she has all the vices of a Republic without a single compensating virtue; for she is no more fitted by her manners, her traditions, or the genius of her people to be a Republic, than is Heaven. In grasping at liberty for all, she has secured license for some thousands of little tyrants who are let loose all over the country. And while I am upon this ungrateful and melancholy subject, let me declare my belief that perfect liberty is impossible, and no Republic can make it possible. I will take the United States as an example of the best working Republic. Well, in the United States: it is true you may vote for a President; but you are compelled to vote for one of two men who have been chosen by two conventions with whose formation probably you have had practically nothing to do. You may not like either candidate, but that makes no difference: you must take one or the other,—or indeed you are at liberty not to vote at all. Now, an absolute Tzar, if he be in a cordial mood, may say to a province:—I am sending down to be your Governor Count X. and General Z. You may choose either, but one of the two you shall have. In the Republic, that cordial Tzar is represented by a small body of men who work the political machine and talk about freedom. Of the two, I prefer to live under the autocrat, and entrust my well-being to a man who springs from a race of kings, whose family has had the large traditions of rule, and who has learned to be a king, as other men learn to be tinkers, or what you will. Neither would I lament, but on the contrary greatly rejoice, if kings were empowered to abolish their prating foolish Parliaments which offer no protection or advantage to be compared with that which men might derive, I do not say from the judgment and mercy, for they are qualities which could be greater or less in different reigns, but from what is common to all,—the tradition, education, and sense of responsibility of an absolute monarch. And sure I am that a holier virtue streams from the anointed hands of kings, than from the frock-coat of any Republican."

He got up, walked to the window, and stood drumming on the glass for a little, and then proceeded:—"I have told you, I lay a good while at Rome. My reason for resting so long there was not that I was better pleased with the state of Italy, than with other countries, but I was introduced to a few so-called Nihilist Clubs, which seemed to be moving in the right direction. I soon found, however, that the members, so far from being thorough moral Nihilists, were not even sound in theory. They were simply vermin, without the least force of character, who had not the courage to do what they pleased, and who let all kinds of childish prejudices defraud them of the pleasures of the moment. The very sight of the unspeakable dolts whom again and again they elected presidents, made me ill: those men might as well have been mayors of provincial towns, and were as timid as provincial tradesmen."

"They never elected you, I gather," said Mr Vellery demurely.

"No; I have already hinted that they gave me no reason to respect their intelligence. It was humanity at its weakest gesture. But a matter far more important is, that during my intercourse with these clubs I noticed the working of the spell, or more properly the curse, which has been the blight of my existence.

"This curse I am now to explain. You must know I am unable to think intently upon any scheme, to plan the details of any action, without finding, at most within a week, generally within forty-eight hours, that my plan has been reflected on another brain, and my action carried out by another hand, in some part of the world. My power of mental concentration is, I suppose, so vigorous, that other minds attract the thoughts to which they have affinity, that are shed from mine. From this knowledge has come of late an increased and troublesome responsibility I feel as to my thoughts; for I have the certitude that my thoughts, even against my wishes, will be materialized. For example, some years ago I was used to variegate my leisure with the devising and elaboration of amusing conceits, such as the explosion of public buildings, or the destruction of arsenals, or again, the removal by fire or steel of a capitalist; but when I found upon opening a newspaper a few days later, that the deed had actually been committed, and that the executor was being hunted as a malefactor, I tell you frankly it gave me pause."

"Let us hope so," said Mr Vellery.

Argan looked at him gloomily for a moment, and was in two minds to start a row over the pious interjection; but he thought better of it, and went on as though the other had no more than sneezed.

"That, however," he said, "was not the worst. Thoughts of that kind I could easily control, and they were of no importance to myself; but when it became manifest that all my cherished plans, excogitated with hardship, and contrived to make me illustrious, were conveyed to the brains of other men and by them carried out, the matter waxed serious, and even outrageous. I may, perhaps, have a great intellect, and a certain store of generosity; but it appears an error of generosity to supply, without murmuring, inspiration to a great part of the human race."

"It makes a man like Burton's *Anatomy of Melancholy*," quoth Mr Vellery.

"You are in the right of it," replied Argan, whom the remark had fallen wide of by several yards. "It does make a man sour and melancholy, and a prey to just wrath withal,—which is the hardest kind of wrath to support. Many a time have I walked to one of those clubs in Rome, and there heard a scheme which I had meditated in the solitude of my chamber, enunciated with an unseemly flourish by some florid orator who was applauded by the blockheads and dotards sitting round the table. At length, tired of such affronts, I abandoned those clubs: and as they have no longer my thoughts to batten on, and I never allow my mind to dwell for a second upon any motion which would be for their good, but on the contrary, pertinaciously desire their confusion, they are probably reduced, by now, to wallow in drivel. Nevertheless, move where I would my hostile fate still clung to me, and does to this day: and a galling result of it is that not one of the plans conceived and inspired by me, is put in act with half of the brilliancy and precision wherewith I could execute it myself if men would but give me time. Look for a moment at the affair of the steamer. The captain did indeed wreck his ship, but three men, as I told you, were saved; whereas, if I had wrecked the ship not a man would have escaped. Again, there is that book of Palleul's: *Études sur la Pratique Révolutionnaire*. The plan of that book I had complete in my head, and was about to put pen to paper, when lo! it appeared in Paris. But what a travesty of my work! what a mass of spongy and unclarified thought! I know Palleul, and he is a dear good fellow, but his book is the production of this brain."

"Surely not Palleul!" exclaimed Mr Vellery. "I have looked into Palleul's book, and heard it discussed, and I am sure that his notions about every subject under the sun are fundamentally different from the opinions which I collect from this conversation are held by you."

The other gave him a long stare. "My good Vellery," he said blandly and yet finally, "I tell you—*I* know the man."

"That obviously settles it," Mr Vellery hastened to respond with a smile. "Henceforth I am dumb."

"There was another book writ three or four years since, whereof the matter was largely the fruit of my intellectuals; but for the manner, and mode of presentation, and the ornaments, those I yield readily to the author. This wight called his book by some fantastical name I have forgot; and he infused into the matter a kind of literary style and finished decoration I despise as useless, and moreover he writ in a vein of irony I condemn as foolish: for who detects and understands irony? But I dwell lightly on my wrongs in the case of books, whereto, after all, I attach but little importance; for I look upon the pretentious airs which authors give themselves, especially in an age, such as the present, overrun with scribblers, when every man and woman who can read a book can, in a fashion, write one, as both licentious and absurd. Yes,—and in the meanwhile, notwithstanding the assumptions and affectations of authors, with the world at large the business of writing is falling steadily into contempt. This has been brought about partly through the incompetence of some, but chiefly through the number of practitioners; because the public thinks (and it has reason) that what so many can do without effort must be facile, and therefore contemptible. And the army of authors will certainly increase, since no one believes nowadays that any special training, such as is required to play the piano, or to paint a picture, is needed to write a book; but on the contrary, most people look upon book-making as a little easier than acting, and a little harder (because more sheer physical strength is demanded) than writing a letter: and so if the fit takes them to get through a rainy day, or a convalescence, or a frost, or other dull time by the divertisement of making a novel, down they sit and make one. Now, as from these reasons I look for a great increasing supply of authors, men and women, I think it will come to pass after another ten or fifteen years, that an author will no more dream of claiming the public esteem on account of his trade, than a fish-monger. Even as it is, it needs more courage for a man to acknowledge in a general company that he is a poet, than to proclaim himself a drunkard;—nay, if he cannot clothe his character of poet with some pretty habit of drunkenness or drugs, or some martial habit of shooting, or golf-playing, to show 'tis a man, he must be taken by all for a mawkish, insipid ninny, and would do better to hold his peace about his toyings with the Muse."

"The ancients," said Mr Vellery, "if I remember right, held that Apollo dwelt on one peak of Parnassus, and Bacchus on the other."

"Did they?" said Argan. "Well, Apollo has come discredited with age; he passes his time now on the peak of Bacchus to have the other's countenance in facing the world. But we have talked enough of writings," he cried abruptly. "Authors are of no importance to me—"

"I'm sure very few of them are to me," put in Mr Vellery.

"And the bare thought of them," resumed Argan, "save those who write useful works such as arithmetics, geographies, or volumes of surgery, makes me dismal. Let us chaunt a somewhat loftier hymn, let us pursue the catalogue of my lost inventions. My scheme for the minute destruction of cantilever bridges in three of the chief cities of the globe, and in such a way as to insure the complete immunity of the agent, was seized by Ekar and by him carried out; so that be won the applause and became the practical, if not the titular head of all the revolutionary societies in Europe and America. My plan for the magnetization of war ships, whereby collisions and other disasters may be occasioned in times of peace, and a paralysis of manoeuvres in war, has been propounded by an individual with not too much sense who is well-known to me at Vienna. But my darling theory, my project to solve at one blow the troubles created for employers by labourers, and the miseries of the labourers themselves, which is nothing less than to draw the brains, the reflective and sensational parts, from some millions of men and women, without injury to the general health, and then, when they can no longer feel either joy, or sorrow, or any emotion, to feed them well as you would a domestic animal, and set them to do any work you choose by the aid of a mechanism I have invented—that project, that stroke of genius, I say it with tears, is claimed and quarrelled over by Lonzignac, Béthencourt, and Shroeder. Alas, many a time, when a vivid and ingenious idea enters my brain, and shines like a star within my head, do I fall to ingeminate the word 'Stay!'—for well I know that once the idea casts itself upon the aerial plane, the mischief is done, and the credit of it lost to me for ever."

With this, the speaker disposed his head upon his hand, in a posture of afflicted discouragement.

"If I were permitted a remark," said Mr Vellery, "I would suggest that your unhappiness springs from looking on yourself as a man of action. You are really a contemplative man, and those persons you have mentioned who carry out your ideas are the men of action."

The other regarded him with strong disfavour. "Your powers of observation are strangely blunted," he replied, not without a trace of sullenness. "The most casual and unsophisticated speculator can see at once that I am at all points the man of action. The moment I have grasped a plan, I hasten to set it working; but the heavy hand of Fate oppresses me, and some one else always arrives first. I tell you it is a spell—a curse." And once more be hung his head in dejection of spirits.

"I too am under a spell," quoth Mr Vellery with diffidence, to cheer him.

"You are?" inquired Argan with mighty little interest, and perhaps a shade of jealousy.

"It is rather unusual," said Mr Vellery, "but no doubt somebody or other has heard of something like it before. And I confidently expect," continued Mr Vellery, "that if I live to be a hundred and ten, and encounter during my life the most surprising and incomparable adventures, I shall always meet, when I relate one of them, with the gentleman who has heard something like it before."

"What if you do?" answered Argan." The symbol of life is a repeating decimal. The thing to contrive is not to repeat too often with the same figure. Let us bear of your spell."

Thereupon Mr Vellery related his ineffectual efforts to sin. Argan listened with a growing concern, and at the end of the narrative— "I have it!" he cried with his eyes sparkling and all his depression gone. "I have it! You're the very man for me. Put it there, Vellery, my dear son," cried Argan, and seized the hand of his guest. "You want to sin and can't. That's very well. I have my head so full of sins that I don't know what to do with them. That's good too. In designing sins—I don't say in committing them all," he added with a light wave of deprecation; "that is owing to my curse:—but for designing sins to suit every hour of the twenty-four, including meal-times, my equal is not to be found on earth. And note that I do not shirk meal-times,—the hours devoted by the family to innocent if perfunctory enjoyment. And for committing too" he reflected with lingering pride, "I don't think I am so far to seek, if I can only get in first ere my notions are stolen. Now, it being granted that I am a shrewd fashioner of sins, and you are an eager and possibly efficient actor, what is still lacking? This: that you be my agent. Into your willing and attentive ear, Vellery, I shall pour my elaborate,—and shall I be thought to boast if I add, sufficiently alarming devices: they strike your brain first, hot, so to speak, from my mind; they rest in your brain, and by consequence do not fly to seek a lodgment in the brains of men to me indifferent if not repugnant. You gain the pleasure, for me," he said, putting his hand on his breast, "the honour. Speak, Vellery, speak, my friend."

"I should like it very much," replied Mr Vellery who glowed with enjoyment at this fair prospect of sin, "if you think I am equal to it."

"Equal to it," cries the other. "Equal to it! Of course you shall be equal to it. I will make it my business to see about that. I'll teach you the trick of it before the next wet night."

"I hinted a doubt," quoth Mr Vellery, "because I have noted that it is only the innocent and light of heart, when they wish to be regarded with awe, who boast of their criminal impulses—those, or men such as Byron, for instance, who brag of their crimes from a sense of youth first, and afterwards perhaps from a sense of humour, but who really have never done very much harm. But the men of strong genuine criminal instincts who wish either from conscience—"

"There is no such thing," Argan put in roughly. "There is no isolated feeling which acts with any certainty that you can lay your finger upon and call conscience. It is all an affair of nerves and digestion. A man feels better or worse about a matter as his health is better or worse. If a man's brain is morbid, it exaggerates and broods; if his brain is healthy, and he has the courage to acknowledge that he has no more free will in the world than a wheel on a cart drawn by a strong horse, he soon perceives that whatever may happen, it is useless to bewail and repent."

Mr Vellery stroked his chin. "'Tis a manner of speaking, this con-science," he said, "and the very name of it influences some. Therefore I say that men who wish, either from conscience or expediency, to stifle their criminal impulses, never speak of their impulses. They are afraid even to think of them. Take the French poet Baudelaire: you have heard of him possibly?"

"I have not," says Argan.

"Well, he was a man of extraordinary criminal impulses: he must often have balanced between sense and madness;—of that no attentive reader of his books can be in doubt. Such being the ease, what did he do? For years he adopted the tenets and frivolous demeanour of the Dandy. After, he forced an interest in ecclesiastical philosophy, and steeped himself in works like that of Joseph de Maistre. By these means he chained and quelled those wild beasts, his instincts, which were ever ready to devour him, till his death; and although he is not formally canonized, and never likely to be, I nevertheless maintain that he is amongst the greatest of saints. For if sanctity consist of deeds, and not of cant, where will you find signs of a more relentless and wearier struggle?—Further, I am convinced that many a man prominent before the world, high in the state, is as much buffeted by criminal impulses as any felon who languishes in a gaol. But he controls these instincts with an iron hand; and not seldom his power is increased by the force of these instincts directed into humane and statutory ways. But as often, alas! the man is so harassed and broken by this ceaseless contest that he has strength left to perform only about half the good work he has projected. If such a man's instincts should once get the upper hand, then his wits run crazy, a disaster ensues, and that is the end. But neither the conquering nor the conquered man ever speaks of his impulses: he leaves that to the happy individuals whose lives run smoothly, who have tranquil nerves, normal brains, and who can discreetly amuse themselves with such fantasies, because they are out of danger. And it is because I belong to this second species, that I have expressed a doubt whether I can be quite the adjutant you wish."

"Console yourself, Vellery," exclaimed Argan heartily. "Encourage yourself! Remember you will have me at your back. You shall come here, or I will meet you elsewhere, almost every day. I shall seldom leave you alone. The moment a project of sin enters my mind—and they come, let me assure you, in battalions—I shall fly to your complaisant ear. I can promise you that some of the sins which I purpose to invent will make the Devil jealous. What is the good of mediocrity in matters of this kind? And if you are tormented by scruples, and not sufficiently disgusted with your fellows, I would invite you to bestow yourself in a park or suburb of any large town on a Sunday, when the citizen with his family takes the air. Look at the ridiculous father, supported by his prolific spouse who presents him with an infant every year, and surrounded by a tribe of children of all sizes, whom he regards with a vain and self-satisfied smirk, and then leers triumphantly at the bystanders, as though to say: You see what a man I am! Look at him carrying the baby, and laughing fatuously with his wife when his eye is nearly poked out by the infant with its rattle. Do you think he and his wife care for the sorrow and misery in store for these creatures they are continually bringing into the world? Do you think either of them heeds that there is a history of alcoholism, mania, or other hereditary disease in one of their families? Not they! Their matter is their own enjoyment: the children, they will say, when they grow up must take care of themselves. Meanwhile, see them roll a rubber ball and laugh boisterously when the poor little wretch who toddles after it falls down and smuts his nose in the asphalt. Yet these are the models of virtue, according to conventional ethics! Ah God," exclaimed Argan spitting into the fire, "what could be more unwholesome and disgusting! And I say to you, Vellery, that just as there are two ways of writing a bawdy book, either to write a book of lecherous adventure, or to write a discourse of chastity; so are there two ways to live dissolute: either to play the common rakehell in lewd courses, or to give a loose to embracements under cover of the sacrament of matrimony."

"This is an uneasy hour," quoth Mr Vellery with a glance at the clock.

Chapter VII

I have no desire to conceal from the patient and obliging reader who has accompanied me thus far in the narrative, that I would gladly put an end to it at this point. For, by my judgment, there will never offer a better opportunity to ring down the curtain than at this moment, when two gentlemen in such dire need of one another to complete and bolster up their characters, as Mr Vellery and Mr Argan, have at last met, and what is more, entered into a compact for their own happiness and for the lasting, though doubtless indirect, good of the public. Gladly, I repeat, would I abandon them in a heartening burst of sunshine, and leave unrecorded the cloudy and portentous matters which are to follow. But as I thought fit, in your interest, to fortify my opinion before acting upon it, I applied to an eminent critic with whom I am slightly acquainted; who, as he was at the time busily engaged upon proving that another eminent critic had never read the books he presumed to criticize, sent me no other response than a lengthy tome writ by a brace of American professors, upon the Physiological and Therapeutical aspects and effects of the Novel. Therein, after toiling woundily through terrible and well nigh impassable bogs and jungles of such extraneous matter as Empirical Idealism; Schelling's Doctrine of Freedom; Pantheism of the Idea: all capitulated by such titles as, The Novel Aperient and the Novel Astringent; the Novel Tonic and the Novel Laxative; the Novel Excitive and the Novel Sedative;—through these and like morasses, I repeat, did I wander with infinite pains for over three precious weeks of this year of God our Lord; till at last I came upon a dogma, hid away between two notes dedicated to the System of Identity, and the Conception of the Moral Organism, which seemed to deal with my business. This dogma laid it down, in a mighty resolute fashion, that a novel is not to be considered complete, or the work of a Master of Art, when it is left in such a state that the reader cannot infer, with the help and goodwill of his imagination, the ultimate fortunes of the characters. Now although I deem it a poor-spirited and mawkish thing for one who bothers his head so little about being a Master of Art as I do, to be started a-marching by two professors I have never set eyes on; still, when I came to reflect that I could neither hold up my right hand and swear, nor lay my left hand over the region of the heart and affirm, that there was a soul on earth save myself who could by guessing come within a league of, far less arrive at, the exact quotient produced from the division of Mr Argan's notions by those of Mr Vellery,—Faith! (said I to myself, striking my hand resolutely on the paper)—'twould be but a sorry trick to play off upon my best friend—who is of course my most interested reader,—to give him an hour's uneasiness (perhaps when he ought to be asleep in his bed), and that merely to show my independence of the two professors, and vent my spleen in return for the miasmas I look in on the barbarous journey they led me. And yet, 'tis the sober truth that at the present I ply but a heavy and uncordial pen: before, there was to relate the inspirations of bright-winged hope, and promises of fulfilment; but now (as the great Addison has it in his elegant verse), now—

> "The dawn is overcast, the morning lowers,
> And heavily in cloud brings on the day,
> The great, th' important day, big with the fate
> Of——"

Mr Vellery and Argan commenced—But come, let us move into another chapter: the air of this is dense enough to give us the vapours.

Chapter VIII

Mr Vellery and Argan commenced their alliance by a dissension so violent as to make it totter to its foundations. This dissension shows the harm that can be done by the importation of private rancours into businesses which are meant to move in the serene atmosphere of abstract principles. The one who disturbed the calm alliance with gusts of passion was, I blush to confess, no other than the framer of it, Argan. And what private rancour did he wish to gratify?—

This.—Two or three nights after his conversation with Mr Vellery, as he was crossing the street in front of a West-End play-house about eleven o'clock, he was knocked down by an empty carriage which was drawing up with a flourish at the door. Argan, although he was half stunned, got to his feet and poured a volley of abuse on the coachman, nor paused to choose terms of cold academical reproof. Thereupon the coachman who had had a glass, not to be outdone, retorted with a loud voice that he drove for the Countess of Quantock, and would run down what people he chose. "It isn't as if you were anybody," says the coachman.

Although in his wanderings through the world Argan had engaged in too many bouts of hard words to be much affected by them; still, as he had a fierce temper which flamed out at a breath, and moreover had just been nearly killed, and insulted into the bargain, be now mounted on the wheel of the carriage with a terrible look, and was proceeding to drag the coachman from the box, when the servants of the theatre who had heard the coachman's vaunt, and knew well that their employer, the manager, would never forgive them if an affront was offered to a Countess's livery before his house, rushed upon Argan, and carried him with scant tenderness to the far corner, where, after many threats, they left him to go his way.

"I appeal to God," cried Argan raising his fists in fury to the dark sky, "I appeal to God if there is any country under Heaven, and ruled by Hell, where the poor man has less chance against the rich and powerful than in this of mine. What is the use of prating about equal laws for all? Oh yes, we are all equal—in the statute books. But owing to the flunkeyism which is rooted in the mass of men, a poor man has really as little chance of redress in this age, as one of the *canaille* in France before the Revolution."

He limped through the streets muttering, and dealt scowls and curses at any passer who offered to look too curiously at his muddy clothes. "We hear a good deal of twaddle, by God! about the liberty of England," he thought as he struck homeward; "but I have never been able to perceive how in the ordinary ways of life a citizen of England is more free than one of any other nation. All England is crushed by the police: an Englishman unless he has a great title, or a great estate, or has been called up to public charges and employments, must rely for his character upon the good will of the police; for there is nothing to prevent a policeman from arresting a calm, peaceable, obscure man, like myself, as he walks the streets innocently at night, holding him in durance till the morning, then dragging him before a magistrate and swearing that he recognized the prisoner in the act of some crime or rantipole; and the magistrate will infallibly believe the policeman. I read not long since that an officer had died of heart failure in the house of a Russian Princess at Moscow, whereupon the Princess had been immediately put under arrest on suspicion of causing the man's death, for she was known to have traffic with the secret societies. Well, whether the fact is true or not, the point for me is that the English scribe who reported it fell to boasting most wantonly of British liberties, and shook with horror when he contemplated any Continental police system. But the plain truth is that if a man were to die under suspicious circumstances at the house of—let us say a Countess, here in England, there would be no prosecution at all, for the influence of her relatives would have the affair hushed up: whereas on the other side, if a man were to die under the same circumstances in the room of a washer-woman in the Kent Road, Polly Soap-Suds must languish in gaol—poor devil!—in this free England till the police had made up their minds whether it would be worth while or not to try her for her life. That's the way things go—that's the benefit we get from the free air of old England! Let me be the Marquess of Quantock who is knocked down, and then see the whole boot-licking staff of yonder theatre run to haul that drunken hound of a coachman to prison. But, you see, my hearty lad, you are only Argan—Labour Argan."

It may be useful, madam, to remind you who are too wise to spoil your looks by a study of the laws, that there was a great deal of injustice in the foregoing vociferation and soliloquy. He forgot that if he had been knocked down before a play-house in Paris or New York by the carriage of some rich and well-known man, he would not have had, in the republican capitals, any better treatment; and the crowd, which had supported him lustily in his row with the coachman, would (so far as my observation serves) have been against him in those two cities. The truth is, that Argan, from his proper infirmities, was unable to perceive the great beauties of Parliamentary Representation, Houses of Representatives, and Chambers of Deputies. Moreover, he was a Nihilist political and moral, and as such was abstracted from the natural state, and course of thinking; wherefore, as he made a mock of patriotism and our usual decencies, and proceeded by methods very different from the ordinary dictates of sense and reason, which dispose you and me to pass our lives in the common forms, he paused not to measure the huffs, kicks, and foul language he applied with equal relish to his own country and the stranger.

The next day, nothing less would do for him but he must present himself about half-past three of a fine afternoon at the Countess of Quantock's house, where he was confronted by a servant whom he astonished by requesting him, in no very amiable tone, to go tell the person who fed him with the offal of servitude, that there was one who wished to have a word with her. The man in his stupor found nothing better than to repeat his set phrase, "Not at home," and was upon closing the door, when the intrepid Argan introduced his leg within the jamb, and drawing a revolver cried with a loud voice, that he would do his business for him if he did not at once take the message. This he rapped out with so violent an emphasis that the servant turned as white as salt, and retreated to the back of the hall, ringing a bell as he went. The bell immediately brought three other men on the scene, who, not observing the revolver (which indeed by this time Argan had restored to his pocket), with remarkable boldness cast themselves upon the intruder, seized him by the shoulders, and projected him into the square. Shuddering with rage and outraged pride, and devoting (rather unreasonably, don't you think?) the entire Quantock family to despite and perdition, Argan hastened to the nearest post-office, and despatched an instant message wherein he asked Mr Vellery to come to him without delay. Mr Vellery arrived in the evening.

"You want to be an eminent sinner, don't you?" said Argan. "You want to commit a good rousing sin?"

"Yes," replied Mr Vellery cheerfully. "That is what I should like."

"Well then," says the other, "here is your affair. In the park at this time of year there is a great concourse of carriages of an afternoon, and the carriages move very close together. Now you are to station yourself to-morrow on the path which runs by that part of the road where the carriages are thickest. You will be armed with a small weapon which I shall provide; and it will be no other than a small air-pistol constructed to discharge six poisoned needles at a shot. This weapon which, for the rest, is so small that it can be used without danger of detection, you will discharge at a pair of horses belonging to a person I shall specify. The horses, maddened by the pain, will plunge and then bolt: the people in the carriage and the driver of it must infallibly be killed: and when I consider the crush, I entertain strong hopes that other horses will take fright, and by consequence a great number of swaggering, chicken-brained scoundrels, and easy overfed women,—fair ladies, by God!—will come to their deaths."

"But that will be murder," quoth Mr Vellery faintly.

"Let us not employ terms which are tainted with prejudice," responded Argan. "Surely you are not weak enough to feel compunction in stamping out a few mature and seasoned butterflies of women, who while they drive, throw conquering looks upon the common earth in the fond imagination that every man they pass is dying with desire for them; or in sweeping from the road a few men amongst the most coxcombical and offensive you can find. A man with an assured, self-satisfied look, is a perpetual affront in a world so full of disappointment and misery. If you be prosperous, the least you can do is to confine your contented smirks to the privacy of your chamber, and see to it they do not outrage the haunted eyes of the wretched and the outcast. Far from jibbing at murder, whenever I see men or women smiling insolently, wallowing in ignoble conceit of themselves, I feel the desire to slash that smile from their faces with a knife. Why, give me the chance, and

I wouldn't pause to take them off while they dreamed." Then, when he had given Mr Vellery time to swallow this genial and pastoral sentiment, our man continued:—"To be sure, in this business there are the horses to be thought of, and they must be considered as victims immolated for the general good: I trust that not many of them will come to harm. The carriage I wish you to mark, belongs to a woman who goes by the name of Countess of Quantock."

"What, you don't mean Lady Quantock!" cried Mr Vellery in extreme surprise. "Why, I have known her since I was a child."

"The less chance there is that you'll miss her then," replied Argan drily. "She keeps good horses, as I have reason to know;" and he went on to relate his mishap at the theatre. "Now, Vellery," he ended, "what have you to say?"

"What have I to say?" repeated Mr Vellery. "I wonder you can ask such a question. I refuse, of course."

Argan darted a subtle venomous look. "You refuse of course! That's your present song, is it? My excellent Vellery," he sneered, "I would invite you to devote in future your somewhat tenuous faculty of sinning to studied absence from church, or to pulling the hair of your little nieces, if you have any. There is a certain strength of backbone in your character which I took account of the first night I met you, and I think you would be successful in such enterprises,—I do truly."

"You may say what you like," stoutly answered Mr Vellery. "I would assuredly like to commit a sin, and to feel I had committed one completely. I make the most gigantic efforts to arrive at that end: it is the chief reason, if you will allow me to say so, that I am in your company. But when it comes to taking the life of an old woman who has never done any harm to anybody, but who has, to my knowledge, done a great deal of good,—well! I must say I decline. She probably hasn't heard a word about the doings of her dog of a coachman. Now, if you are bent on murder," continued Mr Vellery in a lighter strain, "I wish you would exercise your art upon a man I met at lunch the other day, at the house of the lady whose novels you admire so much—Mrs Ardour. His name is Horace Rear,* and a more unspeakable animal—"

---

* Of Rear, and of Mrs Ardour too, the reader will find an impartial account further on in this work.

"I never heard of him," interposed Argan harshly and uncivilly. "If he is an enemy of yours, you had better undertake him yourself. He will have a long life. Here is your hat, Vellery," says Argan, giving it to him. "If you stay longer things may be said that neither of us will patiently hear. I am disappointed in you, Vellery; my pride must own that—bitterly disappointed. You promised (nay, by God, you did; 'tis no use to shake your head), you promised to bring me renown by the execution of my schemes, whence illustration would have fallen on yourself. At the first step you shy. You are a failure; you have put away the chance of fame. Farewell!"

Chapter IX

Chaste stars!

Be not startled, sir, too wide-awake from that state of balmy somnolence which 'tis good for your health to be in, when in an hour of unbuttoned ease you open a book, by the abrupt violence of this apostrophe. It is but the proem or first note of a sounding rhetorical address, which (as I follow the best classical models) I am now to make to the astral luminaries.

Chaste stars! If—

But upon second thoughts, I deem it well to abandon my stellar appeal, because if you cannot have it, you will, after the manner of men and women (for in this you and I are on a level with our neighbours) think a vast deal more of it than if you should find it here under your hand, albeit embellished with the best ornaments of speech I could manufacture. Besides, 'tis after all but a florid and troublesome way of saying, that of the whole chapter of foolish and poisonous brawls in which the sons of Adam indesinently engage, surely a brangling dispute between two men whose interests are tied up in the same box is the foolishest and most poisonous.

The obvious truth we have just agreed upon together, marched into Mr Vellery's brain with a sound of trumpets and flying colours a few days after his quarrel with Argan; and once enthroned it became tyrannical. Under its dominion he fell mopish and uneasy; the opportunity of garish sin seemed, after touching him for an instant, to have slipped through his hands into a deeper, more remote well than ever. In this dismal mood he paid a visit to Lady Quantock. His friend, as he expected, was completely ignorant of her coachman's signal bullying and over-driving qualities: indeed, she showed what to some will doubtless appear a most unjust anger against that worthy, and so inadequately appreciated his fine loose tongue, and boastings in the public street of the pride and gratification he derived from her service (even as a knight adventurous at tourney and joust was wont proudly to give forth his lady's name), and the contempt wherewith it inspired him of low folk who went on foot;—these transcendent qualities, which receive due and valuable recognition from so many modern wealthy families who, though they have nine-tenths of the gifts which life has to offer, do nevertheless manifest a curious uneasiness lest the world remain ignorant of their importance, and therefore reward the dependant who proclaims it the loudest, were held, let me repeat it, in so slight an esteem by Mr Vellery's friend, and struck so cold upon her imagination, that she turned off the coachman without more ado. She was, in fact, so much distressed at the accident, that she asked Mr Vellery to explain to Argan how sorry she was it had come about through the clumsiness of her servant. This message Mr Vellery eagerly promised to deliver, for he perceived that he could use it as a flag of truce to arrive at an armistice and negotiate a peace. Accordingly, under cover of the message, he presented himself at Argan's lodgings before the week was out.

Argan, meanwhile, had been dull. His virulent rage against Lady Quantock had quickly evaporated; for it was a characteristic of his temper that if the wrath which such injuries inspired him with had no immediate outlet, it never hardened into steadfast malignity; but contrariwise, other schemes thronging into his head not concerned with any individual, put revenge out of doors. He had only one rancourous thought left as to Lady Quantock now; and it was, that she had been the cause of his contention with Mr Vellery. For, as I say, his head was thick with plans; to eject them by speech would have given him ease; and he missed the sympathetic attention of his disciple. From this it will be plain that few apparitions could have contented him more than the sight of Mr Vellery in his room: but he chose to throw over his pleasure a veil of grave austerity, and sat as though he plied his book, though he was not reading a word.

"Well, Vellery," he said slightly, still with an eye on his book, "so you have struggled from the marble palaces you frequent to this poor abode."

"Yes, I've managed to cut my way through," answered Mr Vellery with a smile. "I bring you a message from Lady Quantock."

When he had given it, "Sit down, Vellery," quoth the other, who was no longer able to conceal his satisfaction. "There is no need for you to use your legs in this room while I have a chair left. Perhaps you will even share my humble beverage. I have been low of late, Vellery; bitterly low. I will aver to you, my dear sir, that I have, in my tribulation, called upon the bottle, that I have, in short, endeavoured to drink my spirits high with brandy; but the result," he added gloomily, "has not been commensurate with the excellence of the means. When you put a quarrel on me, Vellery, (yes, yes, I swear 'twas you began it!) about a mere nothing, a trifle, a bone to fling to a dog, the pain—but let us talk no more about it; let it pass and be forgotten. Your angry words are now become for me as the dead leaves that fall upon a man's coat who goes through a grey wood, when the wind rises in autumn, in the evening.—A far more cheerful theme happily attends our conversation. I have of late brought to perfection a plan, which though the particulars of it may strike a casual examiner as but drab and commonplace, will nevertheless, I am assured, leave with the perpetrator an exhilarating sense of crime. Now, friend, are you for Paris?"

"Yes, I will go if you like," replied Mr Vellery. "I have nothing to do just now."

"Good! now listen. You have read in the newspapers, if you share any of my interest in such matters, that the great Calvados railway company wishes to employ a new kind of connecting passenger coach, based on the American system; and consequently intends to run a special train made up of these coaches as an experiment, so that the prominent French and English financiers, who will be invited to go on the train, may be in a position to judge for themselves. A great deal of the wealth of Europe, to speak in a figure, will be upon that train, Vellery. Now, one of the chief English share-holders in the Calvados is Sir Hugh Anger, who is, I have learned, your uncle."

"Not at all," said Mr Vellery a little troubled. "Nothing of the kind. A distant relation—simply that."

"All right, Vellery; the farther off the better," replied Argan jocosely. "In the business we are now on, what with your tender feelings, and one or two other matters, we can't keep social relationships too far out of sight. But the good lies in the fact, that you can easily get permission through Sir Hugh to travel with the train. Once aboard the train, when you are about an hour out of Paris, and moving at a high rate of speed, you will pick out the car wherein are seated the greatest number of capitalists, deposit in that a small case I shall give you, and immediately retire through the train till you come to the wagon-restaurant, which will be on the end; and there you will remain till the progress of the train is terminated by an explosion. According to my calculations, the coach you put the case in will be blown to pieces; but the other coaches will not suffer much damage—which seems rather a pity, when I consider the number of financiers who must escape. You, in the last carriage, will be completely safe,—except," he added, as an afterthought,—"except from the chances of death which lie in derailment, or in explosions other than that provoked by me. And I seriously hope there will be no death from these causes,—not out of any weak humane emotion, but because I would wish to reflect that all the deaths which happen on this glorious occasion are to be certainly attributed to my handiwork. That is all, I think. Shall I give you the case?"

Mr Vellery thought and thought, looking miserably distressed.

"Come, Vellery, play the man," cried Argan with a loud encouraging voice. "Why, Vellery, my son, you're not going to shirk, are you? Vellery, Vellery, don't kill me with disappointment."

"Give me the case," Mr Vellery said at last in a low tone. "It's dreadful—dreadful, but I suppose all sin will seem to me like that, and I must begin some time. I am certain to die of remorse when the thing is done: however, that will be a new feeling. The only decent feature in the whole dastardly business is that I run a good chance of being killed myself. Still, I would have preferred some other kind of sin."

"Man, man," Argan cried out reprovingly, "what language is this to hold! Stiffen your brain; shake clear of prejudice. Social morality is no more than doing what we don't like, and saying what we don't mean. You lament at a great moment, in the tone of a school-girl caught cribbing her lesson, and with as little reason for it, you condescend to a similar hyperbole." He was, however, too pleased at the promise he had got, and with it the anticipation of the excitement which a successful issue of his contrivance would cause in Europe, to care much about Mr Vellery's comminatory phrases. "It is now half-past four," he went on. "The special train leaves Paris to-morrow afternoon at a quarter-to-two. You will have time to see your relative (let me again express my satisfaction that he is not an uncle), and to catch the night mail at Charing Cross. And, Vellery, let me beseech you, if you find your energies grow feeble, to remember that you hold in your hands the reputation of—shall I be thought vain if I say, a man of genius?" And with that he stroked his brow somewhat affectedly with one hand, and held out the other to his companion.

Here, to maintain the moral purpose of this narrative, and to discourage legerity and flighty imaginations, I did purpose to write a Chapter of Behaviour, compacted in the form of a sermon, wherein for the better explication of the matter, I intended to observe these particulars;—

First, That a man who wishes to sin must be a very innocent man indeed.

Secondly, That it is a grave error in one who desires to sin, to seek the aid of another man, instead of leaving himself, with a trusting heart, entirely in the hands of the Devil; and this because the other man will commonly propose sins for which his client hath but little stomach. And,

Thirdly, and lastly, Something inferred from both the former, to wit, that in sinning, he succeeds best who makes the least effort to succeed.

This weighty business, I repeat, I was in train to undertake, and had, indeed, hastily written over five or six rough sheets, when I found my thoughts crowding so eager and thick, that what with prologue, divisions and sub-divisions, points and counter-points, deductions, conclusion minatory, conclusion hortatory, conclusion of encouragement, and conclusion salutary, together with the peroration, I could never manage to deal with such a mass of abstruse reasoning in any less time than a twelve-month, or in narrower space than is compassed by a volume. Moreover, such is not to-day my humour. To-day the sun is shining; the wind sweet and gentle, and blows a soft gale which confuses the leaves; the birds are gaily building in the hedges; the new-dropt lambs are jumping on the hillocks and butting their brothers to show what fine strong fellows they are, just like a boy come home after his first term at school—yes, and the blue noisy streams are running and chattering like mad: on such a day, prithee, am I in a mood to demonstrate, or you to be persuaded? Nay, let be! let be!—I'll lock up my sermon till some grey misty afternoon congenial to sober meditation, and give you a glimpse at it when we meet again. Wherefore, for these very good reasons, I shall no longer tarry upon abstract reflections, but rather invite your attention to events of great importance which I mean to rehearse in the chapter ensuing.

Chapter X

Mr Vellery, having weakly consented lest he and Argan should once more go together by the ears, and also to rid himself of the oppression of innocence, delayed not to seek his kinsman; and having obtained what he wanted, set out for Paris the same night.

The next morning, about noon, as he was sauntering in no easy mood through the streets, he fell in with a friend who invited him to lunch at a neighbouring restaurant. He accepted with a febrile eagerness, plucking up his spirits, the while, to meet ends with his company: and they had sat long together in pleasant conversation, when Mr Vellery started up with a bewildered look, and pulled his watch from his pocket.

"By heaven!" he exclaimed, "the train is gone."

"What train?" asked his friend. "Are you going away this afternoon?"

"I am going to England to-night," answered Mr Vellery with a low countenance. "There is nothing now to keep me here."

Accordingly, in great dejection of mind he left Paris as soon as he could. Nor had his spirits become brighter when he compelled himself to face Argan. But how amazed and suspended he was when he found that one all sore and bruised, his arm in a sling, and his head swathed in bandages!

"What has happened?" he gasped.

"You see before you, Vellery," responded Argan with a bitter smile, "the remains of a man. The train—"

"I regret to report," says Mr Vellery, trying to carry the affair in a tone of jest, "that the business of the train didn't come off, as they say."

"Didn't come off!" roared Argan in a wonderful loud voice for a man so battered. "How can you stand there and repeat nonsense like that, when you have in front of your eyes the living proof that it did come off!"

"I don't understand," said Mr Vellery, hebetated. "I tell you, I never put my foot on the train at all."

"Oh that!" cried Argan, as though calling his mind back with difficulty to some forgotten transaction. "Your train! Nothing, I confess, was farther from my thoughts. I was speaking of my own train.—You must know, that the day after we parted, about half-past one or two of the afternoon, I went a small journey by rail to an unattractive suburb. My sole companion in the carriage was a man of plaintive and crouching aspect, dressed in rusty black, with a mourning band on his hat, whose looks naturally filled me with vivid apprehension. This man alighted at a station; and the train had hardly proceeded a quarter of a mile without him when a terrific detonation saluted my ears, and I was hurled violently to the floor. The windows of the compartment were smashed; fragments entered my head and hands; and I was removed by alarmed officials in a dazed and mangled condition. I have since learned, that by the malice of Fate, no one else on the train received the least injury."

"You must have been blown up just about the time I should have been exploding the millionaires," said Mr Vellery nervously.

"What has that got to do with it?" asked the other with temper. "I am neither superstitious, nor an idolater, nor a Romanist. If you waste yourself on such vanities as an attempt to make three and three equal seven, or to draw inferences from the fortuitous concurrence of events, you will have little strength left for other enterprises. No mental process is more debauching. What you failed to do, cannot possibly have had any effect upon what a malevolent scoundrel did do. I wonder, Vellery, that instead of maundering about trifles, you don't bend your not inactive brain to consider how we can be revenged on that ruffian with the band on his hat,—who doubtless in a refinement of cruelty which I cannot but admire, wears mourning for the people he has killed. Now *I* have thought of revenge, and," quoth Argan with a big oath, "I'll reach the miscreant if I have to kill half London to do it."

"Haven't the police any trace of him?" said Mr Vellery.

"The police!" repeated Argan with strong disrelish and contempt. "The police! That means a few years' hard labour. Tell me, is that due compensation for my shattered and dissipated nerves? Is that a considerable equivalent for my calcined beard? For my flayed and morphewed visage? How can you be so childish! My chief hope is, rather, that the police will not find a clue, but let me prevent the hand of the law upon him. I have matured a plan which is sure to touch him sooner or later;

and when it does, he won't blow up any more railway-carriages. I shall need your assistance, Vellery to carry out this plan. Are you game? It will give you a chance to commit a beautiful sin, by-the-bye."

"Of course I'm game," replied Mr Vellery with heartiness. "I don't think it would be much of a sin to attack such an unwholesome dog. On the contrary, it would put society under an obligation."

"Why," says the other, who was a little surprised at the goodwill which Mr Vellery put into this speech, "I am glad to find you so thorough: it is a pleasant change. My plan, such as it is (and I fancy that few brains besides mine could conceive it), like many masterpieces is divinely simple, and can be explained in a few words. You have noticed those advertisements in the form of leaflets which are distributed by "sandwich-men" and others to the passers in the street. All are annoyed by the pertinacity of these missionaries; but hardly one man or woman in fifty is so free of curiosity as not to accept the paper when it is offered. Now, I have prepared a number of these leaflets which I have powdered with a fine poison intended to rub off on the hands of the receiver. The reason is plain. Many people (a far greater number than you, Vellery, who live in a narrow and artificial circle will readily believe)—many people, I say, sit down to their meals who neglect the preliminary rite of washing their hands. Let this be granted, and it is clear that anybody who accepts one of my papers and then sits down to eat without washing, must poison whatever morsels he conveys to his mouth with his fingers. Now it is you I have chosen from many men who would be eager to participate in a work of genius—I have chosen you to distribute my leaflets. Disguised in the habiliments of a mendicant, you will situate yourself in one of the great thoroughfares, and to every man you see in mourning with a band on his hat you will present a paper. By these means I hope to come at the caitiff who endeavoured to explode me: even as great conquerors, after first destroying a peasantry, at length touch the head of the state. Well," he went on, giving Mr Vellery a keen look, "you don't seem very brisk. What's the matter? You were eager enough a minute ago."

"It is different from what I thought," replied Mr Vellery astonished and disordered. "It seems a rather indirect way, doesn't it?"

"You have given me your promise, Vellery," said Argan in a heavy, sorrowful voice. "You see me here all mauled and reduced. Don't, I beseech you, increase the fever of my wounds by a refusal which will upset the dearest project of my life. You, too, of all men—you who desire to be a sinner!"

"Very well," cried Mr Vellery desperately. "I'll do it. This is far more infamous than the train scheme; and if you forget this one as easily as you seem to have done the other, you have a disposition of mind that I envy."

"You always lose your temper in these crises, Vellery," observed Argan: "I have noticed that, and I would point out that it is a mistake. 'Tis purely for your own good I do so. When an Englishman loses his temper he becomes red, and flustered, and absurd. It is only people of a Latin race who can lose their tempers with dignity. We have neither the language nor the manners for that kind of enjoyment. May I trouble you, as my arm is crippled, to hand me my tobacco-box before you go? A portmanteau of poisoned leaflets shall be left at your house to-morrow."

And the next morning, while Mr Vellery was at breakfast, a bag containing the papers was brought in. Mr Vellery unpacked the leaflets which were tied in bundles, and sent the bag away. Then for the following three days he employed himself to find the accurate garb of a street beggar. In his perplexity he could think of nothing better than to apply to a man who provided costumes for the theatres, and by him he was furnished with a suit of rags which might be calculated, if clad in them he ever affronted the public gaze, to gather an amazed and jeering crowd. At last, one afternoon, he found himself equipped in all points for the enterprise; and having donned his unsightly garments, he could not subdue, amid his distaste for the work, a fluttering emotion of pride at the excellence of his disguise, All being ready for a start, he looked about to find the leaflets, but these were not anywhere to be seen. He therefore rang the bell, and his servant came in.

"Skinner," said Mr Vellery, "do you know what has become of a lot of advertisements that came here the other day?"

The man could not suppress a slight motion of surprise at the strange aspect of his master, who looked indeed like a bishop who had brought a drunken bout to an unsuccessful conclusion in the coal-hole. "Yes, sir," replied he, "I burned them all on Tuesday. They were advertisements of ladies'—They were ladies' advertisements, sir, and I thought you wouldn't like them lying about as they were no use to you."

Mr Vellery sank into a chair. "That will do," he said faintly. A thought came into his head when the servant was at the door. "I hope you washed your hands, Skinner," he said.

The man paused. "After burning the papers, sir? Yes, sir. They were very dirty papers indeed," says the man, with one meaning afloat in his eye, and another in his head of a different race altogether.

Chapter XI

Even as an ambassador, who has spent himself to maintain peace, heavily wends his way to the Secretary for Foreign Affairs, the bearer of a peremptory message from his nation which will certainly provoke war; even as the commander of a small out-lying post rides into the main camp to announce that his post has been captured by a surprise: so and not otherwise did Mr Vellery proceed to Argan's lodgings with the dire news of his misadventure. He found his acquaintance in bed, looking woefully sick; and although he disliked to afflict him in his already miserable state, be deemed it well, nevertheless, to get rid of his burden at once, and therefore told his story without superfluity of diction.

When he had ended, the sick man regarded him with intolerance, and as Mr Vellery fancied, a new awakening of disgust and dread. "I think it must have been the Devil who brought us acquainted," he exclaimed in a flush of anger. "Since I have known you, everything has gone wrong with me. You come here bewailing you can't sin: I with much toil and energy invent sins for you to commit,—and I daresay I want them committed too; I have the vanity of the inventor. Well, what is the upshot? You don't commit the sins; but somehow or other, for I can't explain it, the sins are carried out in a reduced and stunted fashion, and through your negligence, carried out upon me—of all people in the world! I don't say you do it on purpose; but that's how it is. I have as strong nerves as any man (or at least I had till my dealings with you;) but I'm not ashamed to own I don't want any truck with supernatural powers."

"Oh come, these are only the whimsies of an invalid," said Mr Vellery indulgently. "You will see these matters in a stronger light when you are on your feet again. I thought you said the other day that you weren't superstitious?"

"Don't let us bandy insults," replied the other; "but let me prosecute my history, and do you attend to what has happened. It was on yesterday you purposed to distribute those leaflets, wasn't it? Well, yesterday evening I went forth to get my supper at a modest eating-house in this neighbourhood. It is one of those places where they put five or six strangers at the same table. A man followed me in, and after fumbling about for a minute or two, he seated himself in the chair next to mine. As he had the bread at his elbow, I asked him to let me have it; whereupon, instead of giving me the basket, he picked up a piece in his hand and put it on my plate. Doubtless a delicate person like yourself would have thrown away the bread: but I have led a rough life; I have sailed before the mast, and I am not troubled with a nice stomach; so I ate the bread without making faces. The man beside me whooped and spluttered some soup down his throat at a high rate of speed; then he paid the reckoning and went out. He had not been gone a minute ere I was seized by a most violent sickness; my head seethed, faintness and nausea made me reel, and my heart beat quick and hard. Alas! I recognized the symptoms. I should tell you, that in one of the pockets of my overcoat which I had hung on a peg when I entered the eating-house, were a handkerchief, a pair of knitted gloves, some loose money, and above all, the only one of those leaflets that remained after the bundles had been sent to you. Now, I found, when I had resumed my overcoat by a strenuous effort of will, that the leaflet and handkercher were still in my pocket, while the gloves and money had been withdrawn. What had happened is obvious. The man who had been next to me rifled my coat before he sat down, and as he was groping in the pocket his fingers, questionless, came into contact with the paper and attached the poison. Therefore you will perceive that when he gave me the bread with his naked hand, he conveyed the venom to a defenceless and unsuspecting stranger. But why do I use the word Stranger? Learn, Vellery, that I have kept the most important point of my narration till the end. I had not done more than glance indifferently at the man while he was at table; but as he was going out I gave him a stare. I tell you, sir, he was dressed in rusty black, with a mourning band on his hat."

Mr Vellery clicked with his tongue, and then hummed a bit. "Does that cut on your head pain you much?" quoth he after a pause.

"That is a way of declaring you don't believe me," says the other with a cold laugh. "However, it is not likely that I lie here merely to compose fantasies for your amusement. If I had not known of an antidote last night, you would have been obliged to-day to refer your business with me to my heirs."

"I have no doubt you are ill," answered Mr Vellery, "and I don't doubt either that it has come from meddling with poisons and other drugs. But when you ask me to believe a kind of wild ghost story, and that you are persecuted by spirits, I confess I have not faith enough at home to meet your claim. You would be the first to take my view of the matter, if you were not now a little vapourish from lack of fresh air and exercise. You seem very comfortable, and not half so ill as I feared at first. I will come again in a few days and see how you go on."

"Come or not," shouted Argan at his confederate's back; "but mind, you'll have to shift your gear to another ship: you will get no more sins out of me."

Chapter XII

I dare boldly say, now we have got here, that if I knew of a way which would take me a league about, that way would I follow. For here we are arrived at an issue fraught with such monstrous—yea, and incredible evils and distresses, that I have little courage left for the pursuit. I would very fain, to the end that you and I might get through the business handsomely together, and that I might spare you a series of shocks in the relation, have drawn from the mud at the bottom of my ink-horn, where they are commonly to be found, some of those soft, rotund, and circumlocutory phrases with which your academical writers are wont to lull their readers, and, at the same time, to decorate and balance their page; but I found that such fine garnitures (if indeed I was not deluded in thinking they were ever at my call) had all evaporated in the great heat of last summer; and so now, may it please ye, there is nothing left for it but to present the facts pure and naked as they were born. My only comfortable thought is, that I took the precaution to intone a protasis and solemn melancholy overture to this part of the piece as long ago as Chapter the Seventh, it being the cardinal chapter of the narrative: hence no reader can fairly accuse me of having by some shuffle and underhand trick beguiled him to terrors where he expected delights. And this reminds me, that I would invite all those who are at the trouble to accuse me of an ignorance or neglect of Art, to consider how artfully I struck the note of sorrow in Chapter the Seventh, with my eye all the time on Chapter the Twelfth, lest the reader might be utterly stunned and overwhelmed by a too sudden announcement of grievous news at this juncture.

Because it is at this juncture that the storm, which an attentive reader must have observed, from the plain though not emphatic hints and warnings I have whispered to him as we came along, to have been thickening over Argan ever since that first encounter in the street, is going to break. Now does Destiny, who has been advancing with slow yet relentless strides, as in the ancient drama, gather up her skirts and hasten her steps till she stands by Heaven! just at the back of her victim, and extends a menacing arm above his head. And hesitate and shirk it as I will, I must declare some time or other,—and here as well as anywhere else let me get it over,—That the cause of the storm, and blind impellant of Destiny upon her sinister errand, was Mr Vellery. I have been at some pains to show that he could not actually sin; but this hindrance did not interfere with his power to desire and plan sins,—whereto, in effect, he gave a loose rein. Now about this time, the pitiless fate of Argan ordained that whenever a sin was clearly thought of by Mr Vellery, Argan, although wholly unwilling, and indeed before he had time to reflect, must at once translate Mr Vellery's sin into action; even if at the moment the thought entered Mr Vellery's head, the two men were divided by miles. This is the bare truth of the situation; but the reason of it I don't pretend to determine. Let it suffice us to know that so the matter stood; and after that you will not need to be assured that some of the results were sufficiently grotesque. Examine what follows, I pray you, as particular illustrations of the general position.

One afternoon, as Mr Vellery sauntered in the park, the beautiful Mrs Darinell passed in her carriage, and thereupon Mr Vellery thought, in an idle lukewarm fashion, that he would like to kiss her.

'Tis most natural, and not to be surprised at.

No. But why should Argan at the same hour, in a street in Pimlico, attempt an apple-woman of not less than seventy years with amorous embraces, and be beaten on the head for a notorious rake-helly dog by a passenger in a rusty suit of black, with a mourning band on his hat?

Again,—What more natural than that Mr Vellery, when seated in a country church on a drowsy summer evening listening to a dull protracted sermon, should wile the somnolent, heavy time with the composition of a counter-sermon, or address to the parson. But why, in the name of those great and good Powers who keep our lives clear and steady, does Argan, in London, on the same Sunday, at the same hour, enter a church, and rising in his place during the sermon deliver a noisy scurrilous speech, and be cast forth brawling by the strong men of the congregation, amongst whom (let us be calm!) he has a glimpse of a man in a suit of rusty black, with a mourning band on his hat?

Many other instances could I give of Argan's frantic extravagant acts; but I have neglected to trace the inspiration of them to Mr Vellery with the same precision as I have done in the two already related. I will therefore not longer delay to tell you of an incident which had grave consequences.

Mr Vellery, one morning in Piccadilly, seeing a sneaking fellow clad in black with a band on his hat before a shop window, chanced to say to himself: "I wonder if that is the man who has shaken Argan out of his wits: if so, I would like to beat him on the nose." At the same minute, in St James's Street, Argan went to fisty-cuffs with a portly important gentleman dressed all in mourning who was just stepping out of a club, belaboured him unmercifully, and tugging at the other's beard must have pulled his chin off, if he had not been in his turn knocked down by the club porter. For this outrageous boutade he was carried before a magistrate, and reposited in gaol long enough to ponder thoroughly upon the late course of his life, and clearly to perceive, which he did with passionate amerity, that all his recent misfortunes were to be attributed to Mr Vellery.

On the very day he was set free of prison, he was overturned and wounded by a cab while he was going dismally back to his lodgings;— and as the dice took a quick run against him just then, no sooner was he got home that he heard the house had been robbed in his absence and fifteen pounds of his money stolen. And even as he heard this, he opened a letter which informed him that a solicitor in the north, to whom he entirely trusted his affairs, had defaulted and left him nearly ruined. Thereupon he went out, and came to Mr Vellery's door a deprived, sorry, and furious man.

"It's a shame I have not been to see you," said Mr Vellery. "I have been away: I have just come from the country."

"Have you?" says Argan. "I have just come from gaol." And without giving the other time to swallow that, he peremptorily questioned him, "Who put me, Vellery, in gaol?"

Mr Vellery replied, "The law."

"It's false," quoth the other; "'twas you that put me there, and you shall know it. Will you hear what has come to pass since we parted?"— And then he presently recounted to Mr Vellery, from the beginning to the end, the history of his misfortunes. At the conclusion, "Tell me, Vellery, as you value your honour," he said in a stern tone, "were you in a low, wenching frame of mind on the third of last month?"

Mr Vellery appeared rather harassed. "What a question!" he cried. "How can I tell what mood I was in several weeks ago? I certainly didn't want to kiss apple-women then or any time."

"Perhaps you didn't want to censure clergymen either," sneered Argan with a look of contemptuous ridicule.

"Yes, I do remember that," replied Mr Vellery. "I should never have thought of it again if you had not reminded me."

"You have probably forgotten also that you wanted to beat a man in black," said Argan sourly. "Never mind; I beat him for you."

Mr Vellery looked at him with a friendly interest. "My dear man," he said, "do get the dangerous and foolish notion that my actions have any influence on yours, out of your head as soon as you can. The black man that haunts you is no connection of mine. I would advise you to see one of those doctors who study nerves and things like that. If he says you must rest, and he probably will, I have a little cottage in Hampshire which I use for shooting, and it is at your service. Believe me, your affairs will all come right if you give yourself a chance."

Argan's eyes glittered; but he smiled with a good show of geniality, promised to think about the doctor, and with his civil humour, as Mr Vellery judged, pleasantly regained, he took his leave.

The truth is, he had determined, the darkened, violent man! to kill Mr Vellery; and he thought it wise to keep on terms with him that a fair opportunity might offer for his purpose. Let this deed be accomplished, and his vengeance satisfied upon his enemy, and he cared not what might after happen to himself: for he was persuaded that never again would he enterprise with any success, and that from henceforth he was in life as a man mowing the tide with a scythe. His plan, which he did not choose till he had wandered through various schemes, was to invite Mr Vellery to sup at his lodgings, and there inject some poison into the drink of his guest. When, however, he wrote to invite the destined victim, he received a reply from Mr Vellery who said he was crippled with rheumatism, and would take it as a favour if Argan would come to his house instead. Accordingly, Argan waited upon his acquaintance that same evening; and during his visit he struck out another way to remove Mr Vellery from the earth. For he noticed at the bedside a bottle of medicine, and it occurred to him that he could easily, while moving up and down in an excited whirl of conversation, remove that bottle, and substitute for it a bottle of the same size, containing a liquor of the same colour, but poisoned. Therefore he eagerly promised Mr Vellery, to whom he seemed once more bright and hopeful, to revisit him on the following night.

"I will visit you till you are no more troubled with gout," he said. "Perhaps we may devise a sin: who knows?"

He found it not difficult the next night to put secretly a bottle he had brought in the place of the one by Mr Vellery's bed.—But I like not to dwell on such an abomination,—no, no, I've just remembered myself in time, and I'll not spend a word on it that I can save; for, to let you into a secret, since first I proceeded author, I've had a foison of good reverend beards wagged at me over this very matter; and if they were to catch me now at my bloody businesses—

I had rather not think of it.

Besides, I am not so enamoured of Melpomene as all that comes to. Therefore, to detain your attention on it no longer than I can help, let me declare, without more words, that Argan's crime (save in his foul intent) was still-born. For the bottle which he removed did not, as he had falsely deduced, contain physic, but rather a most strong poisonous acid which Mr Vellery employed to remove the dross and recrement from old coins, whereof he was an amateur. But Argan in ignorance of this, left Mr Vellery's house and walked the streets with great exhilaration and lightness of spirits, as one who fetches a run after casting a burden. Still holding the stolen bottle, he came to the street he lived in; and being wrought, by this time, to a craze of triumph, he was thinking that now his enemy was despatched it might be after all possible, even pleasant and profitable, to persevere with life, when a man in a rusty suit of black, with a mourning band on his hat, staggering drunk, rolled against him with such force that he was cast forward on the pavement, and the bottle, full of poisonous liquid, cut deep into his hand.

Chapter XIII

Mr Vellery some days later being perfectly restored, and not having seen or heard of Argan, determined of a wet morning to make him a visit at his lodgings. Conformably to his resolution, he set out at once; and as he entered the dismal street he saw a shabby hearse standing opposite the door of Argan's house in the rain.

He found the landlady in the passage and immediately mentioned the name of Argan.

"Yes, sir," answered the woman promptly, and her face brightened. "There's plenty of time to see him. They haven't put him in the coffin yet—they're having a glass of beer in the kitchen first."

Mr Vellery stood lost and astounded in fear and wonder. "It can never be true!" he exclaimed. "My good woman, do please be careful of what you say. You don't mean that your lodger, Mr Argan, is dead?"

"But didn't you know? Did you just come to see him ordinary? Oh deary me," cried the landlady, "did ever body hear the like! Why, he's been dead two days, and they're just going to take him to the cimingtery, and I thought you was come for the funeral, and I was so glad because there's nobody to go with him—nobody in the world.—He comes in here some nights ago with his arm all bleeding, and I met him on the stairs. 'Are you hurt?' says I calm-like, not to anger him. 'Nothing to speak of,' he says, and goes into his room lookin' as white as the grave—well, that ain't very white neither. You see, sir, he was one of them persons you can never get a word to. Well, he never stirred out for three days, and when I went in to do the room I saw him in bed lookin' so bad that I took it on myself to send for the doctor—I did indeed. The doctor comes down after seein' him, and he says to me, 'That's a dead lodger,' he says with a cough,—poor man he *had* a bad cough,—that's just the way he said it, coughing all the time. 'He's poisoned his blood,' says the doctor, or words to those effects. Well, that very same night, just after I'd been thinkin' of buying a carpet for the first floor back and was droppin' into a nice sleep, I heard him groanin'—oh awful. 'Let him take it or leave it,' I says, 'but I'll go down and get him a cup of tea!' But Lord bless you, sir, when I got in he was far away gone. 'Here,' says I, 'sit up and take a cup of nice tea.' But he only looks at me hard and said three or four times, 'It's all Fullery,' he says, 'it's all Bill Fullery!' Them was his words, which I could swear to before the Bible."

The landlady paused, and Mr Vellery had time to meditate upon the numberless errors which must have crept into history from the inexactness of reporters; for he was as certain as if he had stood at the bedside that Argan had said, "It's all Vellery."

"The lay-preacher on the top floor," pursued the landlady, "asked me did he swear and talk drunken, for he says he has often heard him swear, and knew he drank, and what a man does in his life he'll do at his death. But he didn't: be never said a word, nor did no more than moan and say that about Fullery. Well, dear heart! when he wouldn't take the tea I saw he was going, so I turned back the coverlet and made up the bed that he might die respectable like. There he lay for three hours with his eyes turned up, breathing like a train. It did seem lonesome dying like that without a body to speak to except me; and he hadn't given me more than a good-day in two years, so I was only an ordinary friend, so to speak. So just between three and four I went to the foot of the bed and I says to him, to put heart in him, you know, 'Cheer up,' I says, 'you're not dead yet;' and then I saw he was dead. I found the address of his sister in a drawer, and I sent a telegram with my own money, but I never got an answer. That's why we waited to put him in his coffin, because I thought some of his relations might be here; but nobody seems to want to come. Excuse me, sir, but I thought you came to bury him. Now that you are here, would you like to see him before you go?"

Mr Vellery hesitated a moment.

"He don't look bad," said the landlady, "only solemn."

"Of course I will see him," replied Mr Vellery hastily, and grew hot with shame and anger because he had hesitated. He followed the landlady upstairs and into a room where the body of Argan was disposed on a bed. They both stood for a little, silent.

There was a child in the house about five years old, little Job, with a big head and large weary eyes. He now came into the room holding a dirty rag doll in his little dirty arms, and stared for a long time at the figure on the bed. "Is that Mister Man?" says Job.

Poor little Job! He was not her own child, the landlady explained, but her husband's child by his first wife. He sat in a back room all day by himself nodding his big head and playing in a lonesome way with his doll and two broken soldiers, and he was Argan's only friend.

"He used to call him Job Mouse," said the landlady.

Mr Vellery was touched by this sign of gentleness in one who had appeared, and wished to appear so hard, and he looked with new pity at the body of the solitary, forsaken man.

"I don't like to mention it," remarked the landlady; "It isn't as if there was anybody belonging to him to say it to,—but though he never owed me a penny till the last two months, still he left me, as you may say—"

"Oh, as for that—" said Mr Vellery.

Section III

OF FRIENDS

Chapter I

WHETHER THE SUN WAS up of a morning, or the rain came about in squalls, you might see Nicolas (if you were in the village) with Hester, not by his side, but lagging a bit behind, go down the street and take a way to the fields. In truth, he could be nothing but the butt and mark of a small place; for he had a clean pale face all shaven, and hair somewhat long for a man; and he wore a wide grey cloak which came nearly to his heels, a hat made high of hard felt, and a loose tie the ends whereof were taken by the wind over his shoulders. Sometimes, in winter, there would be a meet of Mr Vellery's fox-hounds at the Cross as he went by; and then the gentlemen on horse-back would stare with a mighty pleasant curiosity at this ambulatory figure, and at the pretty sweet face, yet serious, of the woman who went in his company. Nicolas always walked at a good deliberate pace, with his head thrown back and his shoulders full square; and he carried in his hand a stick which he swung round and round, but at times he struck with it on the ground. Hester had to step out briskly to keep up with him; for he never loitered for her, and would throw his talk back for her to catch and reply, like in a game of ball. As she wanted above all things to hear his talk, and to put in an answer at the right time so that he would not be puzzled when he expected one, you will rightly think that she made her feet do their best. Five miles, and seven, and often ten miles they would go in a day; and then back through the village to their tiny cottage at the far end. If they passed on their return a few straggling red-coated hunters, returning home mud-laden from the chase, Nicolas would rail at them to Hester for sottish and ignorant fools.

"They can't see what I am, Hester," he would say, and beat on the road with his stick. "But I'll show them some day. They have the money to ride poor horses to death, and just enough sense not to break their own necks, and that's all."

Indeed, he could not bear any sight which he thought could draw Hester's admiration from himself; and this drove him to these obvious contrivances of abuse. Once when they encountered the pack in full cry, and he caught Hester staring bemused and delighted at the gay and busy congregation, he fell into such a dudgeon that he did not give her a word for two days. On the second night, after she had washed the plates and cleaned things, Hester fell a-crying without much noise in the corner of their little room; and because he hated to see her cry, for he thought how sorry he would be after she was dead that he had ever made her cry, he took a swallow of his indignation and with much circumstance forgave her.

"I am the fox that those people hunt down," he said with an awkward pathos; but she, who saw what he meant, and believed it, threw her arms round his shoulders and sobbed and sobbed.

The cottage where this scene had place, and wherein was spent a good piece of their lives, was of the kind that good farmers commonly give to the labourers who work on their land. Here to Hester fell all the lowly work, such as to clean the floor and cook the meals. Always on their return from the walks abroad, Hester would kneel down serenely to light the fire, with her hair in tangles about her dear, calm face, coloured to a strange beauty by the wind. Nicolas meanwhile would fall into a chair, and watching her would say, waving his hand with a slow smile:

"There will be no more of this, Hester, when I am great."

His belief in himself was indeed of small things the most extraordinary. Although he had passed his fortieth year, an age when the general man is more given to count what he has already won than to begin the game, he attributed his continual low estate only to the stupidity and bad faith of dullards and knaves whom he was confident he would bring sharply and in little time to admiration and order. To speak truly, he lived (if I may use this phrase) on the outside: Reality with her sodden finger had touched him not at all: he regarded his life with the nicest and most sedulous curiosity, as you might watch a mummer's show. Men and women were to him but puppets who made part of the pageant;—either as enemies capitulated against him, or ready to make a leg and raise a cheer when at last he should come forth in his strength. Himself he enjoyed as another man might enjoy a statue, or a picture, or, to come to a closer figure, the adventures of a ship tossed by a stormy sea. That he was a visionary and dreamer more than ordinary, you will allow; and yet it was as a man of action and turbulent mover of nations that he took himself, to the point that he was quite off the hinges when some passer told him that he had the eyes and gesture of a poet, and would not be comforted till he discovered that Napoleon too had been called, in his turn, a poet. And thus he observed not the lapse of years: he played one day Napoleon, another Caesar, another Cromwell, and yet another Bismarck; never was he his own self, and he would have been put to it to find that: but these continual mummeries really carried him along and helped him to live. And it was in a humour of declaiming as Caesar, or Cromwell, or some dead sovereign and politic man, that day by day he chimed into Hester's ears:—

"Things will be different, you know, Hester, when I am great."

As for Hester, it never came into her head that for the twelve years of their conassociation his state had remained consistently mean, and that by consequence there must be something poor and lacking in a man who contented himself to blame on his fellows the plain fact that throughout that time he had not moved one inch towards a better position. No, she did not criticize, the good Hester! The first time she had seen him she had taken for him at once a fond love; and from this she had never changed or in the least wavered, though by now there was in her love some mixture of the love a mother bears for her persecuted son. When she looked at his face, she did not see the close obstinate brow, the dancing, bewildered eyes which showed like panes of glass the riot and fluctuation within his head, the fanatical nose, the unsteady, rather foolish mouth—I say, that she saw none of these, but only the bravest and handsomest face in the world. She had caught from him some smatch of knowledge concerning his great men; and at night when her hard work was over, yet her hands ever busy with some quelquechoses, she would sit and listen, with a patient and wise attention, while he read. The books of Nicolas were few, and they were: Bourrienne's *Napoleon*, a life of Caesar, Carlyle's book of *Heroes*, and Carlyle's *Cromwell*. From one of these he would read with much vigour for an hour or so; and then at some moving episode of the narrative he would pause, half close the book, and look at Hester with eyes expectant of a comment. And the comment never delayed to come in the sweet fall of her voice:—

"That is just like you, dearest; that is just what you would have done in such a case."

Upon that Nicolas would rise, and stand with a certain swell and consequence before the fire for a few minutes, lost in the meshes of his thoughts. Then, as he saw her fold her work, he would kiss Hester on the forehead with a sigh, and take himself, not unhappily, to bed.

Chapter II

Of a life so denuded of incident there is little to relate. But one incident I deem it not idle to recite, since it is the central incident of the subject I handle.

And thus it all came about. One day as Nicolas by a rare chance was on his walk alone, he encountered upon the road a stout busy-seeming man who carried with him the bustle and savour of large affairs. He was dressed in a way that caught the eye of one used to the common sights of the country: a high town hat was set far back on his head; a frappent pin held his scarf; and his broadcloth coat had a newness and lustre ill-accommodated to the fields. He accosted Nicolas with an overdone civility and at once fell into talk of the elections for Parliament which were then at hand. Nicolas listened to the man with much politeness; and as it was his use to study contemporary politics, because he thought that he would some day be prominent therein, and he had, therefore, the details of the questions before the country well fixed in his head, he took up the chant when the man had stopped, and gave forth his views with a freedom and largeness which set his listener staring. At last, when they were come to a place where their ways parted, the man, having first asked Nicolas for his name and where he lived, which the other very willingly told him, cried out lustily, "You shall hear of me again," and so took his leave.

Sure enough, after three days were spent by Nicolas and Hester in such speculation and curiosity concerning the man as people fall into who live obscurely, and to whom events seldom happen, a letter came for Nicolas from the man himself. The man was, in effect, the election agent of Mr Shawlcoat Vellery who was at that time standing for Parliament; and he asked Nicolas to come and address a political meeting which was to be held in the county town. Now, what words can I use to describe, or describing, how get to be believed the rapture and excitement which this letter cast around Nicolas and Hester? They both judged from this event that men in power had at last become sensible to the worth of Nicolas; and they saw a start in his career. Nicolas composed with great formality his speech, wrote it out in part, and in part dictated it to Hester; and as it was rumoured abroad that a distinguished statesman was to visit the town and address a contrary meeting, Nicolas believed himself to be undertaking a conflict against the greatest champion of the tongue that then lived.

At last the day came for their journey; and within an hour or so after they had set forth, they came to the town. Here they found a large gathering of people: all the inns were full from cellar to garret; and they must be content with a bare little room just under the roof. And after a while came Nicolas's friend, the agent, to bid them to a dinner which was to be given in the Town Hall. To the Hall, accordingly, they repaired at the fixed hour, and there were much remarked by the great company assembled; for Nicolas, as I have before said, had a figure which took the eye, while Hester's lively and spriteful look, and pleasing countenance, drew after her the regards of most of those that were in the room. The table at which they were placed was in a dim end of the Hall where the least significant of the diners were seated; and when Nicolas perceived this, he could hardly swallow for the fret and fume he got into at the slight, as he called it, which had been put upon him. Of course, for the man whose mind is based and edified on philosophy, who has his face to the ages and the high dreadful elements of the universe, for the really great man, the place where he finds himself, even though it be among cook-boys and grooms, is the first place; but to Nicolas such matters came in their concrete force, with all brutality, and he was unable to colliquate and clarify them, and thus see how thin and poor they were in essence. He had another shock and agony, of a piece with this, when the dinner was over. It fell out that there was held an assembly, or informal reception; and to Nicolas's fury, and the amusement of Hester, who had much the strongest will of the two of them, the wives of the small squires of their neighbourhood, full of assurance, displaying airs of amiable superiority, and even the pretentious and rather vulgar wives of the prosperous farmers, who knew their story, greeted Nicolas with icy smiles which they thought to be at once full of condescension, disapproval, and contempt, while they ignored Hester altogether.

"The sheep! the dastards!" raged Nicolas when they got back to their little room. "Filthy drabs who don't know how to spell, and can't write any better than their own yokels! But I'll teach them a thing or two. They'll hum a different tune after they have heard me to-morrow."

But it is a good speech, and one of life and fullness, that To-morrow is ever the trite disappointment of To-day. Upon the morrow, the first thing that Nicolas heard was that he was not to address the great meeting in the hall, but rather an over-flow meeting out of doors; in other words (that the thing may be perspicuously expressed), while Mr Vellery with certain members of Parliament instructed the important electors within, he was to keep the rabble outside patient and amused. Nicolas, when this was explained to him, was at first for going home; but Hester beseeched him so prettily, and the agent so persuaded, that when night came he took his place on the cart, which is your *rostrum* on such occasions, with hardly less of the airs of the orator than he would have worn had he been mounted upon the more decorous platform. There, between two flaring torches he stood up tall, and gaunt, and earnest; and for a good half-hour or more he made a ringing speech, full of worthy eloquence and respectable matter. The crowd listened at first in a suspicious and bantering humour; but it soon was carried beyond itself and began to cheer roundly, which noise drew the attention of numerous ruffians, attached to the other party, who were marauding through the streets in search of a row. These rushed with great violence around the cart wherefrom Nicolas was declaiming, and began to shout and jeer, and cut in two his cherished sentences. From that they got to throwing eggs and stones and mud; and at last, maddened by the persisting of the orator, who stood there before them always straight and defiant, they fair escaladed the cart and pitched him out of it head foremost on the ground. Such was his fall, and it came amid mocks, and trumpetings of laughter, and the shrewd gibes which a mob has ever at the service of the fallen. Hester buffeted her way through the crowd, came to him, picked him up, and seeing that he had the fight knocked out of him, and was in a most dazed and sorry condition, she gently led him away by the arm. And the few people with eyes to search below the surface of faces, and note the strange movement of souls, who saw Hester clinging to his sleeve as they passed through the lighted streets, and looking with wet proud eyes into his dirty blood-stained face, had a sudden momentary revelation of what love is without any carnal element, or hope of ecstasy and reward.

One other event connected with the precedent remains to be related. For, the next morning, while Nicolas kept his bed in the inn, and nursed his bruises and hurt mind, with Hester watching him, word was brought to this last that someone attended her in the common room. She therefore at once descended, much wondering whom it could be; and upon coming in, was met by a portly gentleman of about fifty years, with a look of fine prosperity upon his thick, sensual face, who came forward and introduced himself as a Member of Parliament for a distant borough. Hester, who presently thought he had come on some business for the advancement of Nicolas, received him in her open fearless way with much good nature, and civilly disposed herself to listen. But to speak truly, any thought of Nicolas was of the furthest from my brave gentleman's mind. What had set him upon this march was no more than that he had remarked with a lively interest on the night of the dinner the sunny eyes of Hester, together with her mob of russet hair, her white strong neck, and the perfect and most pleasing harmony of her whole frame; and being, although in years, yet lewdly and licentiously given, he had at once taken his informations about her, and set forth this fine morning for her lodging to try a preliminary bout or passado, and see if his good metal could beat down her guard. Indeed, this second view of her stirred up such desires, that it was not long ere heedless of the inconveniences that might follow, he cast aside all decency and discretion in his behaviour and carriage, and became so wild and outrageous that Hester could be in no doubt of his purpose. And being greatly moved thereat, she told him he might be ashamed to offer her such an affront; and then with much niceness and show of concern, she inquired after the health of the lady she had noticed by his side in the Town Hall.

Upon that the gentleman waxed very angry, and holding out his hand he cried: "How dare you!" Then taking himself up, "You seem to forget," he added in a cold tone, as though it were question of somebody in a separate world, "You seem to forget that you are speaking of my wife."

"And you," says Hester with a fine flush, "you seem to forget that you are not always speaking to her!"—and thereupon stalked (poor Hester!) with great dignity from the room.

Ay, poor Hester! She thought he was gravelled by her speech; but she had not moved him otherwise than to a flustered kind of laugh.

Chapter III

The discouragements of the election made no change in the manners of Nicolas, or in those of his only follower. He continued to attend the time when he would come forth with a definite grandeur; and Hester could not discern in the opposition and altercations which marred the speech, together with all that went before, a warning and parable; but saw therein only an evidence of the injustice and brutality of men. Over these elements Nicolas must one day certainly triumph: yes, she was sure of that! But one evil of his visit to the county town was that he had taken a cold there which, after it had run its course, left him weak. His fanatical and absurd belief in his star led him to scorn all care for his health: he could not believe that his career would be checked by a wrench of disease: and so, as of old he perambulated the fields alike in sunshine and the rudest storms. There came a day, however, when as he was in the act of getting into his coat, he fell down in a swoon.

Hester rushed to pick him up, and with her heart cold and sick from the sudden passion which seized on her, she addressed herself to procure his recovery, and hurried a passing boy for the doctor. The doctor came in about an hour, and examined Nicolas who was now seated in his arm-chair with a look of mortal sickness, but perfectly calm and assured.

"Has he had any excitements in his life?" asked the doctor of Hester when they were outside the door. "I've known him here for a good many years, and he's never been much out of the village, has he?"

"He has always been here," replied Hester. "We are going away soon."

"The reason I asked," the doctor went on, "is because it's a most remarkable thing—quite amazing—but he's in precisely that worn-out state you sometimes find in men who have been engaged for years in great business, or politics, or harassing things like that. He's a very sick man, you know." He scrutinized her for a moment, and when he saw she did not blench, as he was old and sentimental he resumed in a less cordial tone: "I'm glad to see you have too much good sense to allow yourself to be bothered by such disagreeable matters."

Hester looked at him strangely with a dreary smile. "No," she said, and shook her head. "I don't mind things much."

Nicolas, meanwhile, sat in his arm-chair propped with pillows; and after the doctor was gone, he talked to Hester from time to time of his plans. Now there is a merry tale of a sailor who said that no man is afraid to die when his belly is filled with rum; but certainly a head full of conceits will stimulate men to discover a courage not less remarkable than that bestowed by any liquor. Nicolas refused, with a slight indignation, to take to his bed.

"A mere crisis of nerves, Hester," he explained. "A slight attack of nerves. It is curious that such a man as I am should have nerves. It is rather depressing."

As the day waned he still talked of his plans, and Hester, looking and listening, had but the one assuagement, that he would never know he had not time to be great. Then night came, and in the midst thereof, little more or less, she saw that he was at last sleeping peacefully, and herself fell into a doze. From this she was startled by a music outside the window (for it was in the Christmas time), and looking at Nicolas she saw that he was awake too, with a terrible change on his face, and plucking with vain inordinate hands at the rug upon his knees. She cried to the musicians to go for the doctor; and when she turned back into the room she saw that the change on his face had grown deeper, and heard the heavy rattle of his breathing.

Hester knelt on the floor by his chair and held his hand. In his endeavour to gain the world, he had gained one creature to whom he had become the world, and with him, for her, the world was gliding away. She plied her poor stunned wits for a text, a prayer, to sanctify his passing. And suddenly without her will she moaned:—

"Lord, remember me when Thou comest into Thy Kingdom."

Then he smiled, just the ghost of the old pompous smile. "Yes," he said wearily, "I will remember you, Hester."

Section IV

OF ENEMIES

Chapter I

To WRITE THE ADVENTURES of writers seems but a pitiful thing; for it is acknowledged that vivid heroism, or romantic adventure, can seldom be the lot of him who sets words in a line. Romance is for those who draw swords, or make treaties, or study the changing visages of kings. Still, tragedies can be enacted in slippers; and the humour of the led-captain sometimes is captured by the pen-man. In countries where military prowess and rapid and glaring action alone win the general approbation, 'tis not amiss now and then to contemplate the quarrels and pleasures of the obscure. Charles Baudelaire complained, that in France in his time, all the metaphors wore cavalry moustaches: and he added that this habit of military metaphors, was an evidence of a people not at all martial, but of a people made for discipline, for the average, who could think only when they were grouped. But in that, I venture to say, the poet was wrong; for where you find these war-like sentiments and phrases most rife, here in our western climes, it is pretty generally agreed that civilization has by now been produced to its most exquisite point: thus I take it, that the mass of English and Americans are more occupied with the words, menaces, and apparatus of war than, say, the Persians, because they are more civilized; and the Germans than the Chinese, I suppose from the same reason. However that may be, we are now come to such a pass in the civilized parts of the earth, that the word Peace, even in church, sluggishly is heard, and scornfully is tolerated. That portion of the globe which is still for con-venience called Christendom, is become, in truth, Pagan; the heroic virtues which were commonly deemed the most important in the great era of Paganism, are the virtues now most valued by the polite nations. To these virtues Christianity tried to give a second place: but never, at any time, did it have entire success; and today America and most of the European countries have reverted to the Pagan ideal. We shall find the present folk cannot be more vexed and troubled, than to meet with such a peevish madness in one of their fellows, that he needs must prate of meekness and forgiveness. This is a state of affairs which I myself regard with unflinching complacency: sure, the stir of squadrons, the smell of powder, and noise and armament of war, are enough to repay all but the meanest for any trifling advantages which attend a condition of peace. Resolutely do I close my ears (and do you likewise, if you would cut any figure in the world),—I close my ears, I say, to those demoded gospellers who urge, that men who will have none of the Christian teaching in these matters, neither advise themselves well, nor carefully look to their own interest; for (thus argue these zealots with a tiresome perseverance) if a nation be not composed of those who will turn in a breath from their trade to a rifle, if the men to the last man are not fighters with the hand as well as the tongue, then (they declare) the nation must hire and give a back to its bully; it must enjoy the swashbuckler, and support the soldier's heavy weight. Now I intend to sift this question thoroughly, once for all; and reduce to mere chaff and dust these vehement appeals to our consciences—which, to be sure, have enough on their hands of private scuffles, without being bothered by inconvenient reflections on the common-wealth. Besides, if I know anything of the times, these gentlemen might very well spare their expostulations; for just as a rain storm may wet a man disagreeably, though it cannot drive a hole in his head, so the arguments and reproofs of these disturbers can annoy, though they do not convince; and our consciences and considering parts which were easy before they came, will by good luck be as easy when they are gone. As I shall never have a better opportunity than at present to communicate my persuasions, here, then, let us enter upon this inquiry.—And first, I admit that Caesar, in a state of Caesarism, is the one man we can think wholly satisfied. Still, is it not better to be ruled by a stern and ruthless Caesar, than by five or six hundred sloven and supercilious masters, who—But I see you start, and rub your eyes. "What is this!" you cry, with a good show of indignation. "We understood you for adventures, and you drone to us of government."—Marry, that is true; but 'tis not so easy to strike slam into a narrative when you have a thousand things besides justling and nudging in your head; and that's why my pen which (if it may go no further) is pretty hard-mouthed, took a liberty with me: and ran off clean directly contrary to the road I meant to pursue. But now I have taken him in grip; and henceforth I purpose to ride straight to the end. So let's to business.

And first, I would introduce Mrs Ardour. When I knew her, not many years since, she looked about twenty-three, and was about thirty. It chanced one summer afternoon that I found myself at a country railway station, among a party of people who were going in carriages and traps to some house at a distance. After a while, only a group of women and one gloomy man were left; and the women fell to discussing how they should manage between a small wagonette and a closed carriage. At last, when there was but one place left in the wagonette, and the gloomy man was still without a seat, a young girl declared that she wished to go in the wagonette. With that, a lady quickly said to her: "Tu ne vas pas laisser ce monsieur avec nous dans le landau, n'est-ce pas? Il a l'air de vouloir nous dévorer vivantes."* This she said in a clear high voice, with an excellent accent for the French; and the remark itself, together with the manifest air of an assurance that none but she and the girl to whom it was addressed would understand the value of it, startled me to a sudden interest in the speaker. She was a little woman and slender, with a pale face, very pretty; her eyes were large, of a grey-green colour, and she had a mass of black hair. All her motions were graceful, and her deportment serene. That she was dressed very well, even I—who, to be plain, what with the manifold businesses and heart-breaking labours I am constantly engaged upon, have so glazed an eye for the vestments of society that I can just perceive, and no more, we have not gone back to tie-wigs—but even I could see that. It was a dusty, hot day, but not a feather, thus to speak, of her plumage was milled. This was Mrs Ardour.

Afterwards I learned more about her. She was an Australian, who had decided, upon her second journey to England, to live permanently in London. Shrewdly she sought the company of the Australian women who had married well, and held a good position in England, and by great arts and social gifts won their friendship. By them she was brought forward: and after a time she could say, that she knew well the people whom most of the other people want to know. Her hus-

---

* ["You're not going to leave this gentleman with us in the carriage, are you? He seems to want to devour us alive."]

band she kept discreetly at Melbourne; and I never saw him all the years that I had her acquaintance: but she gave her friends sufficient and unanswerable reasons, why it was expedient, and indeed lawful, that she and he should live apart.

In the second year, however, of her English life, she perceived that she must make a change. She saw that what she needed was a new basis, where-from she could repel the lightest hint of patronage, or suggestion that she was but tolerated. Her husband gave her a good sum of money; but she had too much sound burgess sense in her clever little noddle, to attempt a vain rivalry with the wealth and power of her friends. Far other was her decision: Let her friends be rich and of high position in the state; well! she was content to be simply a genius. Having taken this resolution, Mrs Ardour at once commenced author. She was indeed void of all knowledge: but in literature, nowadays, it fares well with the unlearned; and she made a brave show of history with the school text-book, and of theology with the twopenny catechism. She had at her command, besides, a thin stream of acid wit which was liker to the squirting verjuice of an antiquated virgin, than the generous kind which you look for in a married woman. She essayed, therefore, a volume or two, which met with a decent success: and by some, almost as ignorant as herself, who wrote criticisms, she was welcomed; and by her own circle, she was, indeed, as she had expected, all-hailed for a genius. But her wit alas! was not only thin and bitter, it was also not durable; and at the moment which, by your leave, I have settled upon as idoneous to begin this history of an incident in her life,* most strangely had it dwindled, and then permanently dried up. Here were letters from publishers, and others of the race; from Australian editors, American editors, English editors; and Christmas not five months off. What in so critical a situation was an honest lady to do?

---

* For it is but an episode in the life of Mrs Ardour, connected with my subject of Second Fiddles, that I here offer the reader. I may add, that I am not alone in thus detaching a fragment from a great theme: Boswell, for example, printed the *Tour in the Hebrides* ere he gave the *Life* to the world; and Carlyle published *The Diamond Necklace* before *The French Revolution*.

Chapter II

Now, it so fell out, that as Mrs Ardour sat one day in the blackest of
moods, to relieve the heaviness of her thoughts, she carelessly opened,
and languidly examined, a periodical miscellany, which she found on
her table, called *The Flame*. This was an obscure print, issued by an
obscure publisher; and what little encouragement had ever been given
it was now entirely withdrawn: for, as Mrs Ardour saw, the book she
held in her hand was near two months old, and contained a notice from
the editor, which set forth, that there the enterprise made an end. As
she read, amid verses of weak bawdiness, and tales which suggested
that the writers had whispered, "Let us chalk it up and then run away!"
Mrs Ardour found one story which woke her to particular attention.
Not all of it was given, and yet a good piece of unusual length: for that
the editor had lacked, among other things, matter to print, and had
used this tale to fill his gaps, for an experienced eye like Mrs Ardour's
was plain. She read this fragment of a tale with great eagerness, and
when she came to the last word, she put away the book and fell into
a deep meditation. Now, one of the ancient writers, and which one of
them it is, I confess that I cannot at this moment remember; but surely one of them says, that a woman meditates evil when she is musing
alone. Whether this be the truth, or an antique lie, certain it is, that
Mrs Ardour soon ordered her carriage, and was carried to the house of
the mean publisher who had put forth *The Flame*. Here she bought old
copies of the magazine containing parts of the story which had kindled
her interest; and with the tale complete in her hand she returned home,
to read it at leisure.

This story was a sound and diligent work: in it nothing was disordered or slurred; the events were neatly arranged and pleasantly narrated; the style, if not elegant, was respectable; and an educated man
could find traces of a deep and solid learning. But as an astute shop-
keeper by instinct can foretell what wares in the coming season the
public will demand, and sternly rejects what he knows it will not buy;
by such an instinct did Mrs Ardour perceive the faults of this poor tale,
and with such an eye examine its weakness. Here, she thought, was an
excellent plot, which the author had not skill enough to handle. Here,
a passage was what she called morbid, and that the public would never
stand,—though of course she was too well versed in her business not

to perceive that it is some gross form of morbidness (albeit she shirked the word, and employed it as a term of disparagement)—the morbid, hysterical side of love, of battle, of religion, of domestic life, which is demanded and vastly relished by the public, and forms the basis of the books and newspapers most in vogue: there, the incidents were coarse, and they were treated either too broadly, or without the crudeness which gives the impression of raw strength, so dear to the general heart. In this book, there was no facile emotion, no gush, little love; it had no droppings from the blue-books; no account of Drawing-room or Levee; nothing of Parliament, of racing, of shooting; no list of peers; and, besides, no obvious French words. The style, thought Mrs Ardour, was involved and obscure, and lacked the easy freedom, and loose syntax of the newspapers: indeed, its restraint seemed to her, an awkwardness. To be buried in the graveyard of a forgotten miscellany was a righteous fate for such a clumsy tale, and for an author who so little knew how to conciliate the public. The plot, indeed, was worth saving; but it would have to be remade, recast, reshaped. As Mrs Ardour needed a plot, and was in lack of subject matter, she determined, without hesitation, to do this herself.

Accordingly, she produced in a very short time, a book that was near three times as long as the paltry tale it was built upon. Withal, she writ it at bits and starts when she could steal an hour from her social affairs; and at the end, she had wasted less time on it, by a round year, that the unlucky author of the earlier book, whose name, by-the-bye, was Martin Straw, had spent a-cudgelling his brains over his prose. The tale had been given by her a new and glaring colour, and had been set in a new frame: one half of it now was like nothing so much as an ill-composed religious tract; and the other half might have been the conversation of a smart young lady with theatrical proclivities. The novel made a great noise; and came forth in a twelfth edition ere a month was out: the incidents which had given to Straw the most exquisite pains to conceive, were noted by the critics with enthusiasm. As for Plagiarism, you may be sure that there was no whisper of that; for even if we allow that any man or woman who read Mrs Ardour's book, had also read the composure of the worthy Straw, where would one be found with effrontery enough to accuse Mrs Ardour, seated on a throne, of thieving from Straw, who was in the gutter? To compare small things with great, as well might I accuse His Holiness the Pope of stealing his dogmas from my Lord Archbishop of Canterbury.

But as *Lady Macbeth*, ere the murder of *Duncan*, spurred her lagging husband, and with stern counsels and cheerful words urged him to the deed; and then, the murder done, was overtaken by the strangest disorder, fell to walk o' nights, and to see blood spots on her hands; so did it fare with Mrs Ardour. Not that she was troubled, and of this you may be certain, with anything so vain and embarrassing as remorse. No: but about this time she began to think of Straw, whom till her book was published she had not thought of at all, as a man who most offensively stood in her path, and blocked her way. Whether it sprung from the fact that we hate those we have most injured; or whether she had apprehensions that he would make upon her a dire attack, and bring her to public shame; there is no doubt that she came to imagine him a wary and relentless foe. Judge, then, of her perturbation, when she learned from a paper, that Straw had dared to publish his tale with the obscure publisher who has been mentioned. She resolved at once to strike a decisive blow, which would teach the man Straw that it was not wisdom to anger, or otherwise to distress, a woman like herself, beyond what her good nature would permit. Again in the cause of Letters she ordered her carriage; and this time she was driven to the office of the Editor of *The Gymnasium*.

Chapter III

The Gymnasium was a weekly paper, devoted to books and writers, which after a year or more of tremulous existence, was become suddenly prosperous and the augur of the booksellers, who consulted it to learn what they should put in their shops. To this position it had come by a very simple method, which was to praise those who already had been successful, and to condemn every writer with a fresh name. Thus it sustained, and kept in the eye of the public, certain brainless old drivellers, who were big each quarter with one book or other, and had brought forth all their lives long. At times, indeed, it ventured to praise some new writer, such as Mrs Ardour, who as the dullest vendor of books could see must (unless for some grave mischance) become popular: and when the author had in good time caught the town, and the country houses, then it loudly claimed in its jargon, that it had "discovered" that author; and for weeks on end kept up its cackle of triumph. Then did it publish portraits of the man-author, or better still of the she-author: he with his dogs or horses, she with her children or cats, upstairs, downstairs, at the table, in the garden, fishing, hunting, shaving, in the stable, he in his shirt, she in her smock, and finally in the lewd act of composing their own books.

For these labours, some men and women were employed by *The Gymnasium* who were, i' faith, a most unlearned and empty crew: but they were all the better for that, as the reader no doubt perceives: for besides the general truth that those who write much about books, read but little; it were mere folly, for this particular work to be hampered by so clumsy a thing as knowledge, or such a corrective drug as refinement. This rabble was found good enough to perform the task assigned by an old forgotten author as the proper employment of a true, ancient, genuine critic, which is, he says, with a good kind of briskness for a man who had not, after all, the advantage to learn his trade in this age,—"To travel thro' this vast World of Writings; to pursue and hunt those monstrous Faults bred within them; to drag out the lurking errors; to multiply them like Hydra's heads; and rake them together like Augea's Dung."

For the better understanding of what is to follow, the reader ought to know something of the Lord General of this organization, and high Director of its policy, whose name was Horace Rear. Rear, from a draper's shop in Leeds had come to London, with the intention to turn author. He had discovered in himself that knack to spin sentences out of nothing, and tie them in a ragged bundle, which since the effect of the Board Schools has been felt, most of us are ashamed to be without. In London, he scribbled a bit here, and a bit there; and as he was it cunning, smooth-tongued whoreson, cautious, frugal, who never lost a farthing by drink or Venus, and never made an enemy by hard words, he got on so well that he could not only live with cleanliness and a certain comfort in Town, but, also manage a jaunt into the country at Christmas or Easter. Such was his situation, when *The Gymnasium*, after a year or more of sickness, fell into the most languishing state, and at length lay a-dying. Rear, when he perceived this, at once made his way to the owners of the paper, and failed not to tell them that he had an infallible ointment and plaister, which if they would give him leave to apply to their child, would restore it to a sounder condition of health than ever before it had enjoyed. The owners, who thought that their paper surely would die, were not loath to attempt a desperate adventure; and by consequence, they allowed Rear to work as he liked. Within six months he had made good his promise: and further, he caused *The Gymnasium* to attract a kind of folk, who in its dignified, honest days, had never heard its name.

Rear was now arrived at importance: he married a woman with money; and bought a very genteel house in South Kensington. To all this he came, not as you may suppose by any quality having the least relation to genuine literature; but by his sure instinct for barter;— though he was wont to say, ere he smothered his origin, which it was not long till he did, that his clod-headed parents had spoiled a fine genius for letters, when they bred him to a trade. But all his life, music was to him as muslin; and books as baby-linen. He loved to give dinners to those esurient adventurers who wrote for his paper; whom, as he could never get over a habit to look on all things in a commercial way, he was used to call, "the people in his shop": and whether you consider what *The Gymnasium* was, or the temper of those who composed it, that seems a proper and adequate phrase. At these dinners, encompassed by a ring of obsequious listeners, he grew large; bullied and contradicted his guests; and gave forth his opinion on all subjects, from the National Budget, to the Prime Minister's hat. Sometimes, in an easy humour, when the wine had mellowed him, he would speak to a few intimates in a tone which left none uncertain that he hoped to bury his wife: then would he portray the kind of girl he longed to marry, and with much liveliness relate his gallantries. Of a truth he was a mighty fine fellow; though some of the diners, as they strolled away from his house, ventured to whisper under cover of night, that he was grievously hen-pecked by the gaunt, silent woman to whom he owed a good slice of his prosperity.

And even I myself, much against my will, am forced, for the sake of impartial history, to shade this picture of his grandeur in my turn, by confessing that he was prone now and then to make a bad slip. The reader, I am confident, will pardon me if I advance but a single instance of a weakness I publish with reluctance; for it is agreed on all hands that no employment is more debauching than a contemplation too prolonged of the errors and backslidings of the great.—Rear (to come to my story) was one night dining in the company of a dirty-

looking millionaire, who had I don't know what low passion to proceed author and consort with journalists; and also of a middle-aged
lord who had fallen somewhat sorely in the world and found it to his
interest at the moment to endure the sight of Rear at his meals. Rear
knew little or nothing about the millionaire, save that he cherished the
society of writers, which was quite enough to earn him the contempt
of Rear, who indeed took him for an emancipated clerk with an eye on
the novel. Time passed, and the millionaire named some journalist he
had lately met. "I know him, too," cries my lord. "You!" exclaimed Rear,
with a curious instinct which sometimes overcame him when he was
with those he considered his betters, to exalt his importance by calling
his own fish stinking and crying down his own trade: "You!" says he
turning to the lord, and pointing his remark at the other. "Allow me to
wonder by what extraordinary accident *you* happened to meet with a
man of that class"—Upon this back-handed slap in the face, the millionaire looked down with that subtle discreet half smile which a certain one of his forefathers probably had on his lips when he was flouted
on the Rialto and knew he had the bond up his sleeve; played with his
wine glass, and said nothing: but he had taken the measure of Rear,
and for the rest of the evening gave him plenty of sea-room to exhibit,
which I am ashamed to say our man did with amazing wallowings and
flounders, to the diversion of the witnesses, who refused to go to a play
lest they should miss a better performance—However, this was but a
temporary mischance; and I would implore you to forget it when con-
templating the life of so renowned and successful a man.

For his method of dealing with literature, he had ever on his tongue
and his pen the names of certain worthies, Shakespeare, Milton,
Tennyson, Browning, who, he said, had never writ a line which he
would have blotted; and he crushed with his full weight any book he
thought had a smell of France;—a country where, if he had but known
it, he would have found more people in the same story with himself,
than can be produced even in this land. When he set out to damn a
book beyond redemption, he would write, that "it reflected the vices
of a certain modern French school." I was once in his company, when
Pascal was mentioned: "I always avoid," pompously quoth Rear, "the
base kind of French novelist." When this work comes under his hand, it
also he will doubtless condemn, from the usual reason, that it reeks of
Paris; though God knows, and any man or woman with a little knowl-

edge of English beyond the common must know too, that there is not a whiff of France in the fashion of it from the first page to the last.

Chapter IV

As Rear was very unacquainted with the people who make a noise and show in the world, and most heartily wished for the favour of those who touch the society of the Great with one hand, and condescendingly pat literature with the other, he was overjoyed when he heard that Mrs Ardour was on his stairs; and with some tumult he rose to receive her. Mrs Ardour entered, with a smile in her large sweet eyes, and an expression of the most entire cordiality on her face. Withal, there was in her manner a vague charming air of anxiety.

"I feel myself honoured—" Rear somewhat clumsily began.

"I have so wanted to meet you," said Mrs Ardour swiftly, with perfect ease. "I always read *The Gymnasium*, and I think its opinions are so right. It has quite the proper tone. Of course anybody can see, that there is one hand which directs all those able writers of yours. It is really as if you wrote all the articles yourself, isn't it?" said Mrs Ardour.

"It is an honour for me," quoth Rear, who had now recovered from his confusion, "to have your approbation, Mrs Ardour. I have indeed tried, to the best of my ability, to keep our literature from contamination, and to foster it upon the principles which are laid down by Shakespeare, Chaucer, Tennyson, and—and—a—other estimable men. It has been no easy task, Mrs Ardour, not at all an easy task, in an age when so many books are issued which deserve" (says Rear, getting warm) "to be burned by the common hangman. But I may say, that in the midst of my toil, I have always been refreshed by your own works, in which the purity of style, and the admirable little bits of character—"

"You are very good," murmured Mrs Ardour. "We must talk of all this some other time."

It is, of course, a fact well observed, that there is no author to be found in the world, who will interrupt the praises of his own composures, unless he is forced to it by some grave and portentous matter. In this case, Mrs Ardour had purposed to enter on what she was come to do, by praising Rear herself, and listening without heaviness to her own praises; but when she saw the kind of man he was, she was fain to turn her purpose, and to begin at the last part first.

"What you say of the hangman, and all that," she observed, "reminds me of what I came to see you about. The other day, I happened to read a novel which filled me with horror. I think it is the vilest and most pernicious book I have ever read. I at once concluded that it must be crushed, for the good of our literature, and the purity of our homes; and naturally I thought of you who have so much power."

"You flatter me," said Rear; "but I don't think your confidence is misplaced. What is the name of the book?"

"It is written by someone called Straw, and it is published by that wretched man, Shudder, who used to publish *The Flame*. It came into my hands quite by chance. I should like to see it killed," cries Mrs Ardour, tapping the ground with her foot.

"Would you like to review it yourself?" asked Rear blandly. He was too acute not to perceive that some motive, other than a mere concern for literature, was at the bottom of all this energy.

"No—I think not," replied Mrs Ardour, after a slight pause. "It can be done so much better by one of your own contributors who are accustomed to write reviews.—I have heard a great deal about your charming wife," she went on, with apparent irrelevance, "I really should like to call on her, and try to persuade her to bring you to lunch with me next Thursday week. Do you think I might? "She saw that she had a gross man to deal with: she determined to handle him grossly, and therefore she proceeded; "Sir Hugh Anger is coming, and Lord Tarr who has written that great book on the Friendly Islands—oh, and Mr Cubitt, who is an authority on the Army estimates, or something, so you won't be too bored."

"I am sure my wife will be most pleased," said Rear, and for the soul of him could not repress a flush of delight. "I don't remember that abominable book which you mention," he continued. "I don't think it has come under my notice. But we can soon find out." He got up and rang a bell, and upon that a boy appeared.

"Is Mr Voltface in the office?"

"Well, he was here about half-an-hour ago," says the boy, with his eye on the ceiling; "but just this minute he's round the corner at the pub."

"Begone, and find him!" shouted Rear.—"The literary life is full of strange contrasts," he remarked to Mrs Ardour, with an indulgent smile.

In a few minutes, a man with a fat yellow face, and big protruding eyes, who looked as if he wore carpet slippers, put his head in at the door. At a word from Rear, he half walked, half sidled across the room.

"Come in, Voltface, come in!" said Rear. "I want to ask you about a book by a man named Straw. Have we had it?"

"Oh yes," answered Voltface, "we have it. I am doing it for this week's number. I think it is a very good book."

"You do not think it is a good book, Voltface," said Rear ponderously. "You think nothing of the kind. You think it is an indecent book. You think it is one of the worst books you have read this year. You think it is a vile, immoral, and outrageous book. That's what you think, Voltface. You think it's a damned bad book!" says Rear, bringing his hand with a clap on the table.—"Forgive me, Madam," he continued to Mrs Ardour, "but nothing warms me like literature."

Voltface had not read twelve lines of the book, but had spoken it fair because on perceiving Mrs Ardour he had taken her to be the author. Now, seeing how matters were like to go, he began to gather up his mistake as hastily as he could.

"Of course, if you look at it that way, the book is not up to much, when I come to think of it," he remarked cautiously.

"No, it is not up to much, Voltface," replied Rear, "and I am very glad to hear you say so. You must write a review of the book that will teach this Jack Straw, or whatever his name is, to give us no more of his twaddle. Make him go back to his cobbling or tinkering, and let him rot in his country town, or attend to his trade. What business has he to meddle with literature, which has been honoured by such eminent gentlemen of position as a Shakespeare, a Milton, a Tennyson, a—a——"

"A Rear, dear sir," says Mrs Ardour softly.

She retired to her house a victor; for within a week the review appeared. I take leave not to print it here, since most of my readers have doubtless some slight acquaintance in the form of the nauseous and scurrilous kind of criticism; and as for those who have not, so much do I envy their ignorance, that I would no more enlighten them, than I would teach a child how to sin. But towards some atonement for a suppression which may seem a grievous insult to *The Gymnasium*, I make bold to say, that never even in that paper, was a criticism better written: the least rags of decency and restraint were stripped off and flung to the winds, and in his naked savagery the critic floundered through its columns. Poor Straw was kicked, bludgeoned, ridiculed, spat upon, to such a point, that you must have shunned the company of so mean a wretch, had you met him in the street.

Chapter V

A certain philosopher has wisely observed, "That men will believe any-thing at all, provided they are under no obligation to believe it." Hence, it comes that opinions, the most arrogant and monstrous, which deal with the Arts, are gulped down by the public without a wink; since none but the critics who give forth these opinions cares a farthing whether they be swallowed or not: while from the contrary reason, the opinions of the greatest divines upon matters of the highest importance, by the same public are notably shied at, and even positively refused. In the case of books, most people who read at all conclude not without a show of reason, that they pay their critic to think for them, when they buy the sheet he writes in: and as they would consider it the idlest folly to par-take of meats which their physician has warned them will bring on a vile attack of the gout, simply to inquire if the physician be right; in like wise their use is without further question to avoid a book which their critic tells them he can by no means stomach. Armed with their critic's opinion, they cut their way through all contradiction; and having used it so often for a weapon, they come at last to value it as their own.

Thus it happened to Straw and his book. Rear, however, was too good a tactician not to perceive, that although one attack can make an author infamous, fifty can make him notorious: therefore, when he had printed the animadversion which I have mentioned, he was content to engage some critics, his friends, to write a few lines of abuse in other papers; and then patiently to watch the book die. This plan met with so much success, that Mrs Ardour had the satisfaction, upon a visit she paid to the chief book-shops in London some six months after the book had first appeared, to find that in them the name of Straw and of his work were unknown. So encouraged, she made bold to look in upon the little publisher; and from him she learned that just seven copies of the book had been sold. Indeed, she found the unhappy man in a most desponding state; his talk was all of ruin, and of a large family to support. As she was the kindest creature in the world, and had no wish to injure any honest man, she gave him the promise of her next novel;

whereupon he plucked up his spirits, and soon waxed as merry as the best.

Yet, I am unwilling to conceal, that within the short space of three years Straw was discovered, by the sharp eyes of Mrs Ardour, to have put forth two little tales. No other eyes worth mention could have found the least trace of these two tales; but hatred and interest had given Mrs Ardour such a keen eye for Straw, that without difficulty she dragged one story from the purlieus of a Sunday-school print, and the other she found lurking in no likelier a place than a German paper. Mrs Ardour read with great eagerness these stories; and as she now regarded Straw as the last of men, and the insolent robber of her own ideas, she at once undertook to stretch and embroider the two tales, and make from them two long and glittering novels; wherein she so well succeeded, that to this day her sweepings bear a great credit in the world. That was the end of Straw: after the publication of the books his name was no more seen: and I will add, to let you determine how obnubilated, even for Mrs Ardour, he was become, that for six or seven years his name never once came into her head.

Chapter VI

Seven years after the events I have narrated, Mrs Ardour was come to great fame. Her books were read wherever upon this whole Globe of Earth there were any found to read English; she made public speeches which were heard with respect; she was courted, no less for her amiable qualities, than for her pleasing demeanour. Certainly she had enough to content a mind which demands even more from life than she did. It was about this time I first saw her, in the manner I have related at the beginning of this work: and I observed on that occasion, with what deference she was treated. But alas! not long after our meeting she had a fall when hunting with Mr Vellery's hounds, whereby she broke her wrist, and was so much shaken she had to keep her bed. It was while she lay there in sullen impatience, that for the first time in seven years she thought of Straw.

She thought of him with no pleasure, and with little disgust. Her principal feeling was a sharp curiosity to know what kind of man he was; how he lived; and chiefly to know what he thought of her. Not that she had any uneasiness about the sources of her three novels, for she now looked upon them as the inventions of her own genius: but she was anxious to find (such are the silly whimsies which are bred in solitude), if she was held in the same honour by him, as by the rest of the world. Solitude had not been experienced before by Mrs Ardour: for though you may think solitude is needed to produce great works, in that you are mistaken, as I can prove by the case of Mrs Ardour, who never sought retirement when she was making up her novels, and indeed preferred to dictate her prose to a secretary, whom she conversed with upon various light matters in the pauses of the love-scenes. Induced, then, by the morbid and unhealthy emotions which spring from solitude, she determined to seek for Straw; and should she perceive in him a due recognition of her glory, to become his patron. If Straw had ever hectored or complained, the hatred which at first she had for him would have been strengthened: but his silence created her indifference, and in her weak state, her pity. Therefore, as she had never in her life known what it was to resist the least whim or boutade which came into her head, no sooner was she well, than she cast about for the means to advance her design. She wrote to the German editor who had printed Straw's last tale, to ask for the author's address; and received a reply which gave a direction at Paris. Upon that, she made bold to write to Straw himself. She took, however, a very high tone with him; and roundly gave him to understand, that she was Mrs Ardour, and he was but Straw: yet did she show, if he were tractable, she might be well disposed. She waited some three weeks; and at length one morning a packet was put into her hands.

Chapter VII

(*Martin Straw to Mrs Ardour.*)

"Since at last you have broken a silence, which for me at least, has ever been full of the most delicate and comely intercourse, I make bold to send you a brief narrative and abstract of my life. It was written by me in expectation of this time when out ghostly talk should pause, and you most sweetly approach me with living words.

⁓

"In my childhood, scored as it was by paid, and seared by ravening fevers, I felt, though I did not know, that I was cloistered from the world. In youth, I learned that men, for the most part, had no contact with me; and I as little with them: for while they, with much noise and scramble were pushing forward in one direction, I was sidling along the edge of the road, going in the other. Sure, it was by the sorriest of mistakes that I ever landed upon this earth: when my soul started on its perilous journey, it intended to arrive at a different planet; Mars, or Jupiter, or the pallid Saturn star, or Hesper with its dreamy light. Upon the earth, I was like to a sad wanderer in a great foreign city, who will follow the wrong path which lies on the right, while the right path is far away to the left, and so his faultering steps bring him at last to the meanest quarter of the town. Yet, I did not in my youth refuge nor take sanctuary in the shining and fragrant mansions of the poets; but rather envied the deeds of those who put us again to our geography, order armies, and depend upon the drawn sword. In youth we idealize the real; later, we strive to realize the ideal. I was seized, like most dreamers, by the glamour of action; for in this I am like to those who are ever convinced that they are the chosen ones to act, till they find, of a sudden, that other men have acted.

"I stood one evening, amid a snowstorm, in the market place of a village. The snow had fallen all the wild day; and in the evening it came thicker, and rode headlong over the gloomy mountains on the crying gale. The old sexton crossed the place with feeble and uncertain steps, to roll the church bell for one who had just died. Ere it had tolled thrice, a troop of soldiers appeared through the snow, and with sharp words of command, and clang of accoutrements, trampled down the square. My blood was stirred; and I gazed, with my heart beating, and parted lips, till the shadow of the last trooper passed from my sight:—and then the bell was still tolling. Sadly, with a face folded in grief, I entered the church to murmur for the poor wandering soul my forgotten *Requiescat*. This seems to me an allegory of my life.

"It was about the same time, that I first began my attempts at the choice and combination of words. This I undertook with the same sharp interest that a little fellow brings to a game: to pick words as you would flowers; to turn them over with a nice and curious touch; to endeavour that each one should fit exactly in its place in the sentence, seemed to me a noon-day sport and vivid pastime in the sun. I had no thought of fame, and none of money; for I counted the pleasure I had in my task a fair enough reward: so that if one had come to offer me, besides, either fame or money, easily I could have smiled, and answered like to the *Officer* in *The New Atlantis*, 'What, twice paid?' That I had no desire for applause other than my own, was indeed fortunate; since what I have written, for the praise it has had, might as well have continued in my drawer.

"I am come now to the finest and most delicate part of this confession; and it is a part which I should never write, and still less send to you when written, if I were not assured that you and I shall meet on this earth, never. Therefore, it would serve no purpose to let you suppose, that when I found to what a degree your novel was imitated from mine, I was not grievously disturbed. I was, in truth, most angry, to the point that I meditated some retaliation. But one night, when I was in London, I went to a theatre which offered a tragedy, and there was enacted for me the prettiest of comedies. A lady sat in front whose face compelled me more than any face I had seen in my life; and so I sat like a fool, lost to the motions of the players, gazing at her through the long evening. As she rose to go, she dropped her glove, which by good chance I picked up and gave to her. Then one who was there said, 'That is Mrs Ardour.' On my way home, I resolved, that whatever I had done, or in future might do, was not to be mine, but your own; and I thought that when I picked up your glove, I had been afforded by fortune a graceful outward sign of my allegiance. What things in future I was to write, were to be written to carry a cheerful aid and help to your nimbler pen. That you had chosen me was enough delight, when 'twas so rich a pleasure to serve; and sure am I that if you had ever given any token that my service stood remembered, I could have only smiled and fallen to my— 'What, twice paid?' Here in the power to bring you help, was come at last the one reward for my labours that at any time I had craved: but woe is me! no sooner was this sweetest purpose for writing come, than the power to write was itself withdrawn. Since that day I have composed nothing good; and if I were to endeavour, before my task I could sincerely repeat the words of Lamennais: 'J'écrirai avec dégoût, mal par conséquent, et il est triste de s'ennuyer pour ennuyer les autres.'* Nor could I have found a pleasant balsam or tonic in the thought which he

---

* ["I will write with disgust, badly therefore, and it is sad to be bored to annoy others."]

added, 'C'est pourtant l'occupation des trois-quarts des hommes;'†—
since what the three-quarters of mankind do, is what I have striven
all my life not to do. I wrote notwithstanding two little tales, but they
stood in such dark corners that I feared you would never find them; yet
so anxious I was to bring them under your eyes, and do this least part
of my service, that I presently thought to send you the two magazines: I
did not, only because I dreaded that you would not rightly understand
my motive, and therefore be disturbed. But you did find the two stories,
as I learned with exceeding joy: and methinks that hardly you could
have failed to discover them, and use them as your own; since for that
end heartily I had longed, with such fervent wish and prayer.

"Upon this, if you please, I will end. Pleasantly we have spoken
together with our earthly voices, but ere the last word has been said,
we are sure that our commune can have no duration. Now that our
talk has ceased, I look around my mean little room, and deep down in
my heart I know that I am alone, and the loneliness is become a bitter
thing. But the door opens, and the ghost I have known so long for you
comes to me, and takes my hand, and dries the despairing tears on my
face; and then cheerfully we commence again that faint ghostly con-
verse which we knew of old."

Chapter VIII

I have now, with much toil, night-watching, and cogitation, brought the
reader to a place in this work, where without impropriety I can ask him
to consider its importance. For, in my zeal for Literature, which I have
the welfare of so near at heart, I have not only given a general picture
of that calling, but gathered up examples of particular serious votaries,
who, though they may differ among themselves, are all covered by the
decent appellation of Author. Thus, by innuendo and suggestion, I have
enabled the reader to admire at and reverence the genius and writings
of Mrs Ardour; I have intercepted and actually printed a specimen of
Straw; and if I have neglected to take a page and a half from the works
of Rear, that has come about either through lack of space, or through a
nice regard for the canons of Art, which forbade me to drag in his prose
and exhibit it where I would. But lest the reader may grow uneasy at

---

† ["It's the occupation of three-quarters of men."]

this omission, and think a trick has been put upon him, I hasten to add, that as Rear talked so did he write; and we have seen how he talked. Wherefore, through all these merits I think fit to lay hands for myself, here at the end of my book, on the plain and honest title of Author: and I make humbly bold to beseech my honourable good Lords and Ladies the great professed Authors, who in this age are come to such reputation, that they beard kings, unsteady thrones, direct the councils of Europe, and from their homes command armies and puissant navies;—I make bold, I repeat, to beg these illustrious performers, male and female, although I am shamefully conscious my pen was not cut on the same day as their own, to admit me of their company, if only as a collector of the ink, boiling with their inspiration and haste, which amid their huge labours they throw plentifully about: and so by the chance thus given to overhear and gather up the words they murmur over to themselves, I may come to know what they think and design, and thus learn what to avoid, and escape becoming an unwary robber from their Royal Highnesses' mighty ramparts of knowledge. Far as the southern pole may it ever remain from me to put these glorious Masters and Mistresses, by my action, upon restoring a gap in the said ramparts, which would be for them a cruel and vexatious task, and keep them for painful weeks from profitable trade.

Having thus cast off a burden which has plagued me this long time, I have the happiness, with increased lightness and agility, to resume my subject.

We left Mrs Ardour (as the courteous reader cannot easily have forgot) with Straw's letter in her hands. What struck her first was that she could not make head or tail of his brace of quotations: the Frenchman she had never heard of; and as for *The New Atlantis*, after skimming over a list of her rivals' works (which were the only books bless her! she ever bothered her head about) and not finding the name there, she hastened to interrogate Rear, who by this time was grown to great credit among her literary friends—whom, in course, she did not confuse with her other friends. But Rear had never heard of such a thing as a "New Atlantis" in a long life, and was gravelled by her pertinacity almost to death, till he hit upon a story that it was a translation out of the modern Greek which a lady with her reputation to keep up would do well to leave alone.—"And as to this Minnie, or whatever you call him," continued Rear, when through unwillingness that Straw should know what she did not, she put a question with respect to Lamennais;—"Why," says Rear, "as he is a foreigner, he is probably a low adventurer, sprung from we don't know where, whom no Englishman of sound honest British principles would care to have in his house. This between ourselves, dear Madam," he added with a thick smile; "for I am a man of the world, and flatter myself I can treat foreigners when I meet them in a public place with a happy mixture of condescension and ease. But they must not approach those nearest and dearest to us, Mrs Ardour—not the home. The family hearth—and I don't care who hears me say it—is as sacred to me as it was to our immortal bard Shakespeare—whom indeed not a few have told me I resemble."

That much settled, Mrs Ardour proceeded to a consideration of Straw, and before long came to the conclusion that he was little better than a prig: he seemed to her morbid; and his vain talk about writing for the mere delight in it, mighty windy and ridiculous. To her hard practical nature, which I for one cannot regard with enough esteem, he appeared but a futile fellow. Still, she was a little stirred by the devotion of so infirm and helpless a creature; and the incident of the glove, which, of course, had not stayed in her memory, she deemed romantic, and a not inelegant or unpleasant tribute to her power. Further, she was surprised and pleased to find that Straw, instead of proving the huckstering lout, talking loud of his own genius, and snorting for revenge, whom she had dreaded, was, in truth, glad, and counted it a privilege, to give her what she had taken. From this, she came to look on the feeble Straw with pity: she thought that if she were to take him in hand, he might yet be made to frame well. It was one of the principles which had guided her through life that men should be estimated not only by what they are, but by what they have the power, howsoever hidden, to be; not only by what they do, but by what they can possibly do. From all these reflections she decided, in defiance of custom, to go to Paris and make the acquaintance of Straw. As she had no pressing engagements for the next few days, she determined to go at once; and with her admirable decision, she there and then rang the bell for her maid, and gave the order to start.

The next day, as she drove to the house where Straw lived in the Rue Jacob, passing through the clear winter afternoon she began to think not without a slight uneasiness, that she might have ordered the matter with more restraint and decorum. Plainly, the reticent method was to write to Straw and ask him to wait upon her. But a mawkish and maudlin sensibility, which lay deep in her nature, and was indeed largely the cause of her success as a novelist, had on this occasion, although she did not often allow it to cloud her judgment in the affairs of actual life, come to cuffs with her plain sense, kicked that out of doors, and sent her fluttering off on this expedition. Straw had written, as you will remember, that he looked for her ghostly form in his room, or some such rubbish too tedious to repeat (for the present writer confesses that with poetics and maunderings he has little patience),—but the effect of Straw's words had been, to raise a conceit and silly caprice in Mrs Ardour's brain, for the nonce a prey to sensibility, that she would come, unexpected, to Straw in his loneliness, and console him by her real presence. Even now this feeling was so strong, that the disturbing thoughts could make no stand against it; and one after another they were banished. Mrs Ardour, by consequence, felt angelic, and believed she smiled like an angel, when she alighted at the house in the Rue Jacob. She went to the room of the *concierge* and asked for Straw. A girl of about sixteen, who sat there sewing, looked hard at Mrs Ardour, and seemed about to give some information; but she changed her mind, and only murmured that she would find the *concierge*, and so she left her. Mrs Ardour, waiting, fell to an examination of the house. It was stained by the weather, and in places the paint had peeled from the walls; the stairs, she could see, had no carpet, and a sour reek and stench arose from the court.

The *concierge*, a stout woman with a cross whimpled face, bustled in with that air of consequence which a certain kind of French woman always assumes when she thinks she has an important matter to communicate.

"I wish to see Mr Straw," said Mrs Ardour, as the *concierge* waited for her to begin.

"Mr Straw is no longer here, madam," replied the woman curtly. "He has left."

Mrs Ardour was disappointed. "How tiresome!" she said. "Can you give me his new address?"

The woman looked straight into her eyes for a moment as if to gauge her strength; and then—

"He went without leaving his address," she answered. "He is dead."

Mrs Ardour felt that she shot a little pale. She opened her mouth to ask some questions, but she only stammered her thanks, and turned away.

Out in the sunny street, she walked idly for a little, feeling neither glad nor sorry, but a little shocked, as one feels who has just looked on the face of a dead man. The last words she had heard, *He is dead, he is dead*, rang in her head without meaning, like a chime. She stopped, and looked into a flower shop, and there her coachman who had followed her broke her reverie. She told him she wished to walk, and sent the carriage home.

So the man was dead. She knew, by instinct, that he was the one man who had loved her with entire devotion; who would have slaved and become mean for her and have asked no reward; who had looked upon his hand till it became day, as of no value save as it might help her. Never before had she been loved like this, and never again like this would she find love in the world. She realized that such love is not given twice in a lifetime. For the first time in her existence, she felt a sting of conscience, and a touch of sorrow: she would have liked to have had at least the chance to hold his hand; to tell him she was sorry; to hear him say that he forgave. As she thought of these things, her heart swelled, and the tears gathered in her eyes.

She was now come to the Quai, and a cold wind from the river blew upon her face and changed her mood. She noticed, that in a way she had never felt, she was now feeling uncomfortable; and with dread she looked forward to sleepless nights crowded with regret. "I shall not have a good night for a week," she thought. With that she took out her handkerchief to wipe away her tears, but her eyes were already dry.

From these sad reflections she proceeded, as she crossed a bridge, to a resentment against Straw, inasmuch as he had brought upon her all this pain and discomfort, by choosing thus hastily to die. At the Louvre, she was really angry with the dead man, and withdrew her pity from him, that she might commiserate herself.

In this temper of mind, since it is characteristic and final, let us leave her.

Nay, leave her?—Even so, my dear, leave her and the rest of the companions, good or bad. 'Tis somewhat abrupt, and perhaps it were more decent to withdraw upon solemn valedictories, and long holding of your hands, which I own would please me well enough, since to you, for the good favour of your company on these travels, I am more bounden than to any one in the whole world. Truly, had I known when I was in the middle of the book it would be such a wry business, after we had passed several days together, to bow and walk off,—I'll give my other hat if I wouldn't have prolonged the journey by a couple of hours; but who, till he has made an end of much more than a book, and arrived where he can cast a long general review over the dusty miles of life, shall prescribe what continuance were wisdom, what withdrawal; what reticence, what diffusion; whether he should have halted at this place, or at that advanced? But if there be always at such junctures some word or so to offer in behalf of a sudden parting, there's a good deal to be said for it in this case; indeed, I am convinced we might hunt about till next Thursday without finding a better spot to resume our separate roads. And the reason, if you seek one, is just at our elbow: for it is precisely here that we can cry heartily Farewell! and step out of the book with our admiration perfectly exalted, wrought to its highest pitch, and in full working order for the power to raise tempests, over-cloud weaklings, and sweep clean their own path, discovered by Premier Fiddles. They are an irrefragable guild, and till the world grows simple will ever have the last word.

THE END

www.ingramcontent.com/pod-product-compliance
Lightning Source LLC
Chambersburg PA
CBHW061251170626
46809CB00007B/2945